OBJECTS OF DESIRE

OBJECTS OF DESIRE

·

·

·

Stories

Clare Sestanovich

Alfred A. Knopf   New York   2021

THIS IS A BORZOI BOOK PUBLISHED BY ALFRED A. KNOPF

Copyright © 2021 by Clare Sestanovich

All rights reserved. Published in the United States by Alfred A. Knopf, a division of Penguin Random House LLC, New York, and distributed in Canada by Penguin Random House Canada Limited, Toronto.

www.aaknopf.com

Knopf, Borzoi Books, and the colophon are registered trademarks of Penguin Random House LLC.

Library of Congress Cataloging-in-Publication Data
Names: Sestanovich, Clare, 1991– author.
Title: Objects of desire: stories / Clare Sestanovich.
Description: First edition. | New York: Alfred A. Knopf, 2021.
Identifiers: LCCN 2020036263 (print) | LCCN 2020036264 (ebook) |
ISBN 9780593318096 (hardcover) | ISBN 9780593318102 (ebook)
Subjects:
Classification: LCC PS3619.E83 O25 2021 (print) |
LCC PS3619.E83 (ebook) | DDC 813/.6—dc23
LC record available at https://lccn.loc.gov/2020036263
LC ebook record available at https://lccn.loc.gov/2020036264

Jacket design by John Gall

Manufactured in the United States of America

First Edition

For my mother and her mother

CONTENTS

OBJECTS OF DESIRE

ANNUNCIATION

·

The first time she flies home for the holidays, Iris makes two friends. She is seated between a married couple, because the man prefers the window and the woman prefers the aisle, and they are the kind of people, she discovers quickly, with strong preferences. In general, Iris is the kind of person with mild preferences—preferences that can be painlessly ceded to someone else's. When the man clambers over her to use the bathroom, Iris presses her chin against her neck, closes her eyes, doesn't mind at all. The woman follows him a few minutes later, and then Iris is alone in the middle of the row.

She is eighteen, living half a country away from her parents. The college she attends is not large and not cheap. It doesn't have a communications major or a business major or a football team. Her parents agree—and they agree on so little—that this is not their idea of an education.

The man climbs back into his seat in time to decline a meal from the flight attendant. While Iris is peeling back the foil on the various components of her dinner—lasagna, green beans, half a dozen mandarin orange segments swimming in liquid—the woman returns and announces she's pregnant. She reaches across Iris's lap, her sleeve dangling perilously close to an uncovered dish of chocolate mousse, and waves a plastic stick in front of her husband.

"The plus sign!" she says.

"Fuck yeah!" he says.

He covers her hand with his hand, so that they're both holding the stick. Eventually, he lets go and she leans back in her seat. She beams blankly at the postcard-size screen in front of her, where a plane is making slow progress across a map.

"Congratulations," Iris says politely, sawing the green beans in half with a plastic knife.

The husband has brought them both burritos from a famous restaurant in the city they have just departed. Iris has seen pictures of the burritos, because no one goes to the restaurant without documenting them. In real life, they aren't that impressive—overstuffed and milky with sour cream. Black-bean juice dribbles down the wife's hand.

They tell her they've been trying for months. They tell her they like ancient names.

"Theodora."

"Cicero."

They offer her guacamole.

"Are you sure you don't want to sit together?"

Iris chews a tortilla chip as quietly as possible. She wonders if the crunching is really as loud as it sounds in her head.

"Honey," the wife says, "you're part of our moment."

"Marcus," the husband says, wiping salsa from the edge of his mouth. "Or just Aurelius."

Iris's mother meets her at the airport. She's wearing an elegant coat and boots with flower-stem heels, because she disapproves of people who travel in pajamas. The husband and wife tell Iris not to leave without saying goodbye, but she walks away while they're waiting at baggage claim. She looks back once, the wheels of her suitcase clicking in time with her mother's shoes, and she is surprised, seeing them standing together for the first time, that the woman is taller than the man. His arm is wrapped around her waist and she leans in to him, her head resting gently on the top of his.

In the car, Iris tells her mother about the couple. She does not call them her friends, and this feels like losing something—like removing a pebble from her shoe and missing the discomfort. To put the pebble back in would be crazy.

She mentions the baby just as a plane passes overhead, so close she can make out the wheels.

"What?" her mother says over the roaring.

Iris repeats herself.

"They never should have told you that."

The car reaches the top of the ramp onto the highway. The traffic passes them in loud whooshes, and it seems impossible to Iris that they will be able to merge into the stream.

"They shouldn't tell anyone for at least three months. That *baby*"—her mother says this in the voice she reserves for words she does not trust: *the newspaper, the forecast, your father*—"could be gone tomorrow." The car nears the end of the acceleration lane, and for a moment it seems they will have nowhere left to go. Then, Iris can't say how, they are part of the stream. In the mirror, another car has appeared at the top of the ramp, and then it, too, has slipped into the anonymous rush. They speed past unchanging scenery, concrete barriers and spindly trees and a blue tarp in the wind, and Iris feels certain that her mother's words have killed the baby. The car changes lanes. Tomorrow the wife will wake up with a feeling she can't describe, and the husband will tell her it's nothing, it's good, *it's all good*, and Iris, of course, will never see them again.

When Iris is about to graduate from college, she dates a virgin. Exams are over, and no one has anything left to do except go to parties and throw things away. On the sidewalk, there are lamps without lampshades and posters without frames. Iris pushes her bed out the window because it doesn't fit through the door in one piece. She and her friends start drinking in the middle of the day, and by the afternoon, they're half asleep, surrounded by containers of crusted-over hummus and watermelon rinds—cheap ideas of being festive.

The virgin is a boy named Ben.

"But he's rich," Iris's best friend says while they look at him across someone else's backyard.

Charlotte is the first best friend she has ever had. They didn't meet on the first day of school, like some best friends. There was a whole year that Iris endured alone. Charlotte, like Ben, is from Manhattan, where she learned about music and alcohol and deciphering all the signs that money leaves behind. She is the one who told Iris to wear black and white, or else autumnal colors; to drink vinegary brine after shots of vodka; to eat burgers and bagels and bacon—there was nothing, she said, as powerful as eating masculine foods with feminine grace—but to avoid dairy. To wear bras with lace and without flowers, to buy a vibrator, to be grateful, all in all, that she had never been fingered by a teenage boy.

The first kiss with Ben is too cinematic. The sprinklers on the lawn behind them come on the moment his lips touch hers.

"Don't look at me like that," she says.

"Like what?"

Their shoes are getting sprayed. Her socks are damp.

"Like, we're dancing in the moonlight."

He seems a little wounded, and this, somehow, is reassuring.

"Like, this is meant to be."

He closes his eyes for a few seconds and Iris can tell that he is hoping to be someone else—to look, at least, like someone else—when he opens them. She resists the urge to touch his hand, or the smooth skin above his hip.

By the time she meets Ben, Iris has had a lot of sex. Some of it is good and some of it is bad, and she has taught herself not to care too much about the difference. In general, not caring requires studiousness. She gives herself assignments: eat peanut butter straight from the jar, steal ChapStick from CVS. She has dropped acid and skipped class and let a boy lick circles around her asshole. There are dozens of tubes of ChapStick in her sock drawer now, and sometimes she takes them out just to look.

Iris tries to figure out the reason for Ben's virginity, but can't. He is handsome and nice enough. He has accepted most of the other intermediary vices that Iris has learned men like: drinking and smoking and enthusing about oral sex. For a few days, they kiss in places they will one day reminisce about. The library, the quad, the roof of the chapel, where no one is supposed to go and everyone does. She wonders why there isn't a word for the anticipation of nostalgia.

"Do you think I'm cheesy?"

He shakes his head.

The night before graduation, they are naked on Iris's mattress for the first time. She has already packed her sheets and thrown away her pillowcases, which were an embarrassing shade of yellow.

She closes her eyes when he comes, but when she opens them his face is still twisted in the shape of pain and pleasure mixed together. His mouth is open. In the morning, they put on their gowns, and Iris can't find her cap. Her mother will be in the crowd and her father will not and the only pictures she will be in are the ones taken by other people's grandparents.

"Here, take mine," Ben says.

If she had slept well, if she had eaten properly, if she hadn't seen his face in its unknowing shape, she tells herself that this wouldn't have made her cry. He puts his arm around her. She looks at the thumbtack holes in the wall, the pieces of tape she gave up trying to peel away, instead of looking at him. When they say goodbye, what they say is *congratulations*.

. . .

Charlotte teaches her to laugh about it: Iris is pregnant. "A one-night stand with a virgin," she says. "The movie writes itself."

"It wasn't a one-night stand." Iris sounds more defensive than she'd like.

"You know what I mean."

They're living together in Charlotte's childhood bedroom, because they don't have any plans or any money. Until Iris pays a library fee, she doesn't even have a diploma.

"Okay, what's the moral of the story?"

"Abstinence!"

Charlotte's diploma is already on the wall. Beside it, her parents have arranged her school pictures—thirteen years of them—from start to finish. Her bangs grow, her face narrows. Glasses appear and disappear. What Iris likes best is that Charlotte's smile is never the same. She is tight-lipped, then open-mouthed. One year she fakes it and the next year she frowns. She reveals her braces, neon rubber bands and clumps of spit. In the very last one, she wears lipstick the color of an open wound.

Charlotte has a long-distance boyfriend and a metal device in her uterus, both of which require certain stretches of the imagination.

"How can you be sure it's working?" Iris asks.

Her parents leave her favorite foods in the fridge. Her cat scratches the door if she sleeps too late. It's never been hard, she tells Iris, to trust what's real.

"Oh no," Charlotte says, because Iris is crying again.

"My mom doesn't know what my favorite foods are."

"You don't have to laugh about it *now*." Charlotte rubs Iris's back. "We can laugh about it later."

Ben texts her occasionally. Unpunctuated questions, late at night. *What's up. How's life.* She doesn't respond, because the acceptable answers to these questions have nothing to do with her, or with anyone. *Good* or *Okay* or *OK.*

Iris makes herself stop crying, because she isn't exactly sure what she's crying about, and she has vowed, in this new phase of life, to be nothing if not precise.

"*I* don't even know what my favorite foods are."

She pays back Charlotte's parents for the abortion in installments, even though they insist she doesn't have to. She applies for a job because the listing says it requires attention to detail. Mostly, she fixes errors in other people's spreadsheets. When it's time to order lunch for the office, Iris is the one to specify which condiments must go on the side and who is allergic to avocados. Nine months after graduation, she texts Ben—*Hey*—even though she knows she shouldn't. It would be embarrassing to tell Charlotte she's been counting. Ben doesn't respond for two days, and Iris has convinced herself he never will, which makes it possible—easy—to pretend that the text doesn't really exist.

In May, her mother says she's cleaning out the house. She wants the drains snaked, the windows clear enough to fool the birds. Iris's bedroom will be turned into the guest bedroom. The garage will contain nothing but the car.

"You could come home," she says, which is not quite an invitation. "You could help."

Iris doesn't say that it's been years since there were any guests in the house. She arrives with a half-full suitcase and wears the same dress every day. The dress is plain. Blue— almost black.

"You're so pale," her mother says. "Don't wear such dark colors."

The house is the only house Iris has ever lived in. It's a small box on a street with other small boxes. There are minor differences between them, made to carry the significance of major ones. The shrubs are kempt or unkempt, the Christmas lights come down in January or stay up all year, the metal siding is white or grey or faded yellow. Custard, her mother calls it.

She says elegance is a state of mind, Iris texts Charlotte, who lives in California now.

The house is not exactly empty—the furniture is not gone, the walls are not bare—but there is something stale about it, like returning from a long trip, all the usual evidence of wear turned into something ominous: *signs of life.* Had the tile floor always been this cold?

Behind the house, there's a pool with no water and big, prehistoric-seeming cracks along the bottom. Soon, her mother says, she's going to fill the pool with concrete. When Iris was a kid, she didn't like the pool as much as she was supposed to. Her hair turned green and her fingertips shriveled. But she had been good enough at pretending to enjoy it that now—her feet dangling into nothing, the sun burning the backs of her ears—it's almost possible to believe she really had. She's thirsty. Her skin will soon be pink, tender. It seems, for a moment, like a religious thought: that light is also heat.

Iris calls until Charlotte picks up.

"Something happened with her and a man," Iris says.

"She said that?"

"Of course not."

Her mother has never spoken about romance directly. Over the years, there has been a pediatrician and a personal-injury lawyer and a handful of men with big ideas. She never uses the word *boyfriend*. She has sworn never to reveal their ideas.

"The messier her love life, the cleaner her house," Iris explains.

It's barely noon in Los Angeles, but Charlotte is already in a crowd. There are restaurant sounds in the background. The kind of brunch that comes with cocktails. She's there to meet people who are there to meet famous people. It's gauche, she says, to go straight for the top. Iris never says *gauche* because she always forgets how it's pronounced.

"You're being very fatalistic," Charlotte says, sipping something loudly.

Iris lowers herself into the pool. The deep end, but only six or seven feet. Someone says Charlotte's name, cajoling her. Then several people are saying her name, and she's laughing. She has to go.

When Iris hangs up, the phone is covered in sweat. In the middle of the bright white pool, the sun is blinding. There are no leaves on the bottom, no dirt, no mold, no ghostly stains where rain has been. The cracks, when she looks closely, have been scrubbed clean.

Her mother calls from the house, and for a moment Iris feels like a child, hiding. She calls again and a dog barks somewhere in response. The pool is too bright and hot for hiding.

In the evening, they eat a well-balanced meal. Something green and something brown and chicken. Iris's nose is already peeling. She considers the things she might reveal to her mother. The roommate who doesn't believe in monogamy; the coworker who sells cocaine and casts spells; the astrologer who forecast marriage, or usury; the boy who stood above her bed, his eyes closed, still dreaming, and peed all over her sheets. She considers what sort of *pro* her mother is. Choice, life. The options almost make her laugh.

Instead she says, "Are you still dating the entrepreneur?"

Her mother slides a garnish to the edge of her plate. A cherry tomato—for color.

"No, he didn't have his act together."

Years ago, she explains, the man had donated his sperm. Back when they gave you cash, and genetic testing didn't exist. He'd moved around a lot. The sperm ended up in many different states. When he eventually settled down, not too far from where Iris's mother lived, he got married, divorced, married again, divorced again. But he never had any kids.

"The ex-wives all live nearby," Iris's mother says. "He thought, if anything, that his world was getting too small."

By the time she started dating him, the man was online; everyone was.

"And the sons and daughters just kept coming out of the woodwork." She eats the last bite of chicken. The plate is clean, except for the tomato, still whole, which she will throw away.

"Then what?" Iris says. "Did he want to know the kids?"

Her mother places her knife and fork at four o'clock. "*I* didn't want to know."

On the last day of the month, Iris flies back—she doesn't know, now, what flying *home* would mean. The woman between her and the window has a cheery ponytail and a brightly colored backpack. She could be a little older than Iris or a little younger. She starts to say something as soon as their seat belts are fastened. Iris puts her headphones on and smiles blankly. She tells herself she will keep her eyes closed for the entire flight, because this is a test that is both extreme and achievable. She sleeps on and off, and when she is awake, the image that comes to her, accusing her from the backs of her eyelids, is of her mother on her hands and knees, scouring the bottom of the pool.

Iris lives in a room the size of her mattress, in an apartment that belongs to a married couple. She keeps her clothes in a closet in the living room, or lets them pile up on the bed, a stack of unironed dresses like a body beside her. The married couple is in a relationship with another married couple, who live down the street.

"You can ask any questions about how it works," one of the wives says.

"You probably have a lot of questions," the other wife says.

They look at her expectantly, which makes Iris's mind go blank. She shrugs.

Sometimes the couples all assemble in the kitchen. They make elaborate dishes that involve a lot of waiting— slow-cooked meats, twice-risen loaves—or else require speed and perfect timing. Slabs of tuna still pink in the center, chocolate cake that's half liquid inside.

"Who are they trying to impress?" Iris asks Charlotte, who is still on the other side of the country, whose friends, by now, are all semi-famous. Maybe Charlotte is semi-famous, too.

"I love chocolate lava cake."

"Californians don't eat dessert."

"Maybe they're just impressing themselves."

The couples always invite Iris for dinner and mostly she declines, even though she doesn't have anywhere else to be. On those nights, she buys a liter of seltzer and a bag of sunflower seeds from the bodega on the corner. She walks around the city, sucking the salt off the seeds one by one, imagining the decadence of the kitchen. Oven heat, garlic air, sweat and butter, someone's husband with someone else's wife. She cracks the seeds with her teeth and spits. By the time Iris returns, the dishes are piled in the sink, the couples drunk. They say they're happy to see her, which she doesn't really believe. She slinks away to her room.

On New Year's Eve, Charlotte comes home to see her parents. Iris imagines spending the night at their house, a few miles and one bridge away. A dumb movie, champagne in coffee mugs. Instead, Charlotte invites herself over for dinner. She wants to know everything about the couples. Who sleeps in which bed, who pays for which meals, who makes the rules and who breaks them. These are not things Iris has wondered about, but she is embarrassed not to have the answers—her own life made small and incurious in the face of Charlotte's questions.

"Of course," the wife down the hall says. "The more the merrier."

All afternoon, the couples prepare. Iris chops cilantro and watches. They start drinking early, the glasses put down and picked up without looking, the rims smudged with everyone's lips. Soon they're snapping at each other. The garlic should be crushed, not chopped. The oranges should be blood, not navel. The oil pops and sprays and burns someone's wrist. Iris ranks the spouses in order of attractiveness. Or unattractiveness; their faces are all too big. Then she guesses how Charlotte would rank them. When the door buzzes, the couples glare at each other.

"Who is that?" one husband accuses the other.

"It's me," Iris says. "I mean, it's my friend."

They remember. They smooth their aprons. (When, Iris wonders, is the right age to buy an apron?) Someone turns off the oven fan, and it's quieter than it's been all day. The oil crackles benignly.

Charlotte is wearing the perfect black dress. Both wives confirm this. They forbid her from helping and bring her wine in a glass that is not a jar.

"So," Charlotte says, the glass stem held delicately between her fingers, "how did you all meet?"

For a moment, the couples survey the girls from the other side of the counter. Iris resumes chopping, the rhythmic sound of metal on wood filling the silence before their answer arrives.

The week after Charlotte has sex with the married couples—she is already back in L.A., sending pictures of grapefruit from her backyard—Iris falls asleep on the train and wakes up in a neighborhood where old rich people live. All the apartment buildings have names and all the dogs have haircuts. On a street with a wide median, she stares at the map on her phone and swivels back and forth. The blue dot on the screen bobs uncertainly.

Iris walks with no particular goal in mind, crossing to the other side of the street whenever she reaches a red light, so that she never really stops moving, crisscrossing all the way down the city. Iris is imagining the very end of the journey—if she is gone long enough, if her feet hurt enough, if the light above her door is glowing warmly, if her mind is blank with exhaustion, surely it will feel like coming home—when she is stopped short on a corner by the sight of Ben in a suit.

He is standing on the other side of a restaurant window. The restaurant is crowded with people in grey jackets and dark dresses, and there's an old woman leaning against him, clutching him. He doesn't see Iris right away, and when he does, his eyes get wider and his face gets softer. What she feels most of all is guilt. He will wonder how long she's been standing there. He will wonder if his hair is right, his tie straight. He will wonder if it's ever really possible to be unwatched.

"Sorry," she says, but there is a window between them.

When Ben raises his hand to wave, the woman gripping his sleeve looks up. She isn't as old as Iris thought, but her back is hunched and her skin is loose. Without breaking Iris's gaze, she says something to Ben, releases his jacket, stands a little straighter. He hesitates, and she says it again. A command. He vanishes into the crowd of dark clothes, and then, a few seconds later, the door to the restaurant opens and he's standing in front of Iris.

"So."

The walk sign above him turns from white to orange. One last car speeds through the intersection.

"Someone died," she says.

He nods. His grandmother.

"A few more days and she would have been one hundred."

"I admire that."

"Admire what?"

"Like, not bothering to reach the milestone."

Ben laughs and she feels her body relax.

"You'll have to come inside," Ben says. "She insists."

She is his aunt. They sit down at one of the empty tables, with an untouched breadbasket and someone else's purse.

"If you live long enough," she tells Iris, "everyone thinks your mother is your sister."

Ben hovers behind his aunt's chair, but she waves him away.

"Some drinks," she says, and he heads off toward the bar.
The aunt looks at Iris intently. Her eyes are depthless
brown, her eyebrows gone. She kneads a pink packet of
sugar, or fake sugar, between her thumb and index finger.

"He's a good boy."

Iris nods.

"Probably not a great boy."

A few minutes go by, and Ben doesn't come back from
the bar. They wait in silence, or maybe Iris only thinks
they're waiting. Maybe he stopped to talk to his great-uncle
or his great-great-uncle. Maybe he decided to escape. She
wouldn't hold it against him.

"When old people die, they only show you the young
pictures," the aunt says, gesturing around the room.

It's true. There are black-and-white photographs taped
to poster boards all over the restaurant. It reminds Iris of a
science fair. The woman in the photographs has wavy hair
and pretty sundresses. She's lying on a beach, leaning out a
window, holding a baby to her chest.

"They're beautiful pictures," Iris says.

"I didn't even know her then." The aunt tilts the sugar
back and forth. "Our biggest fight was about my wedding
dress."

Iris looks at her sympathetically, and she laughs.

"No, no. Why is fighting always bad?"

The aunt tells Iris that her wedding dress had long
sleeves and a high neck. From the front, it was old-fashioned,
even a little bit ugly, but the back was wide open, all the way
down to her waist. Every inch of skin exposed. Her mother
hated it.

"But it was my consolation prize." Outside, the sky is getting dark. Their reflections begin to appear in the window. "My back looked good. A dancer's posture."

"Consolation for what?"

The aunt frowns at herself in the glass.

"The church was historic," she says, as if she hasn't heard Iris. "In one of those towns where everyone's ancestors came on the *Mayflower*."

She stood at the back of the church and watched all the faces turn toward her. A dramatic pause, so that she could hear the rustling and breathing, and then the organ came to life all at once. She glided down the aisle. In front of her, the faces smiled and nodded, wiped tears or pretended to wipe tears, and behind her, gradually, one row after another, there was a wave of gasps.

"So much skin." The aunt laughs again. "Back then, it was a shock."

For a few seconds, Iris thinks the laughing will become uncontrollable. The sugar is leaking through the pink paper. Her body is a trembling bird. And then, suddenly, it's still.

When they have been quiet for a while, Iris says it again: "Consolation for what?"

The aunt dusts the sugar off her hands.

"Oh, you know." She looks Iris in the face. "The husband, the babies. All that."

Ben appears behind the aunt, clutching three wineglasses in an awkward bouquet. She twists around to look at him. The crenellations of her spine press through her silk dress.

"I was married for fifty years," she says, staring up at him. "Fifty on the dot."

Ben smiles kindly, and Iris can't tell if the aunt smiles back. The windows are nearly opaque now. She has to focus to see the shapes outside—the people walking through her reflection. Iris stands up abruptly, and the glasses in Ben's hands clink.

"It's a long walk home."

"Oh," he says, but he doesn't really look surprised. "Okay."

The aunt turns around. Her face is calm, her hands folded neatly in her lap.

"Don't spill, Benjamin."

He puts the wine down carefully. She bends over in her chair, her chin nearly touching the tablecloth, and blows. The sugar scatters.

BY DESIGN

·

Her son and his future wife took Suzanne out to lunch and asked her to do the wedding invitations. Not so long ago, she had been a successful graphic designer. Her own boss. They were anxious to make her feel useful. When the food arrived, it was vegetables sliced in long, nearly see-through strips, a pile of ribbons in orange and green and red.

Suzanne saw her son's ulterior motive clearly. Being unemployed, she had told several friends, was sharpening her perception. But Spencer took pride in being subtle—probably someone had led him to believe this was the same as being adult.

Suzanne's aesthetic was elegant and inoffensive. Occasionally a little too austere.

"As you may recall," she told the future wife, piling carrot shavings onto her fork, "I didn't lose my job because of bad taste."

The future wife was named Allegra. She reminded Suzanne of a well-bred dog—a whippet, maybe. She had very clear skin and managed to look dressed-up in jeans. Her purse had many small pockets inside; she could always find what she was looking for.

"Oh," Allegra said, a little taken aback. "We like your taste."

When the plates had been cleared, Spencer smiled placidly and signaled the waiter for the check. This gesture disgusted Suzanne. His finger raised almost imperceptibly, the quickest flash of a smirk. If only she had told him how disgusting it was when she had the chance, when he was still young enough to acquire aversions.

"Children are so puritanical," Suzanne said wistfully.

They gave her a few sample invitations for inspiration. Cy and Julep, Booker and Tolu—all the names looked fake. When they stood up from the table, she resented them for masking their relief.

Suzanne had delayed getting married. After Spencer was born, she and Jeb took pride in their informal tribe: lived in a cheap bungalow, pursued impractical degrees, said their plants were their children, too. What difference would a wedding make?

When Spencer was two, walking and suddenly talking, Suzanne had a miscarriage. She knew this wasn't extraordinary—later, she looked up the statistics—but there was more blood than she expected. On the way to the doctor, the towel underneath her turned dark red and smelled. The nurses were reassuring. She could try again.

For years, she had wanted to try everything. Parasailing

and acupuncture, Buddhism and Judaism and art school. Peppercorns that made your lips numb and drugs that made you puke until your life began again. She wanted to live in Patagonia and then in Beijing, because they were almost precisely antipodes. There was a tunnel through the earth between them; just start digging.

Her friends rolled their eyes. Her mother said, *Slow down*. Her mother said, *You can't take an infant camping*.

A few months after the miscarriage, Suzanne and Jeb's neighbor went into labor. The neighbor's husband called before they went to the hospital: the other kids needed dinner, baths. He told Suzanne which books they liked, which toothpaste they wouldn't swallow, which one wanted the door left open and which one wanted it closed.

She couldn't bring herself to do it. Jeb went instead. Suzanne watched him cross the street, then watched him through the windows. Someone else's kitchen, someone else's children, someone else's warm yellow light. He made macaroni and he did the dishes. She willed him to look up, but he didn't.

Suzanne avoided the neighbor after that. *Be nice*, Jeb said—and she was. She waved from the driveway, she left a bag of zucchini on the front porch when she knew they weren't home. The garden was overrun with zucchini.

"I'm exhausted," she told Jeb. She read somewhere that the average American family had 1.5 kids. "That's us."

He frowned slightly, didn't say anything.

"Isn't that enough?" she asked.

Their wedding was just a dinner party in the backyard. Suzanne carried a baby monitor until Spencer fell asleep, then left it among the hors d'oeuvres—the sound of breathing beside the cheese plate. The childless guests got stoned, and the ones with babysitters waiting at home brought side dishes: salads with bottled dressings, homemade dips with store-bought chips. Everyone had half the energy they required. Suzanne wore a skirt—not white.

When the party was over, Suzanne and Jeb went to bed without cleaning up, had sex with their shirts on. In the morning, the house smelled like wine and salsa. They scraped the crusted dishes and put scented candles out of Spencer's reach, grateful for the pleasure of minor transformation.

They were vague about what they expected from a long-term union. At first—secretly—Suzanne was enamored with anything legally binding. She thought of glue. She liked the idea of adhering to someone.

Jeb started paying an accountant to do the taxes. There was never any time for the garden, so he bought supermarket herbs in plastic packages that were impossible to open. Jeb said marriage took work, and he didn't mind when the work was boring. Suzanne stayed late at the office. She went to the gym because she liked to feel her heart pounding in her throat. After important meetings, adrenaline made her confident and restless and she kept forgetting to eat lunch.

Suzanne started the design firm and Jeb almost got his Ph.D. She planned the summer vacations and he did the back-to-school shopping. She paid for both, but no one ever mentioned that. He started rolling joints at night, to help him sleep. Eventually he started rolling them in the morning, too.

Suzanne would never have guessed there would be so

many occasions to say *my husband*. Presumably there were just as many to say *my wife*. But these were the words they used most of all in each other's absence, so it never stopped being strange to hear them spoken aloud.

They spent years delegating tasks—my wife made the reservation, my husband is running late—and then Spencer left and they were alone.

Spencer graduated from college, and Suzanne tried to ignore the fact that she was jealous. When was the last time she'd reached a milestone? A distinguished professor in a tasseled robe said, *The future awaits you,* and she felt left out. She knew she was supposed to feel proud.

Spencer rented an apartment in a nearby city and called more often. In his newly independent life, he had a lot of questions. Do you refrigerate soy sauce? Can you lie to your boss's wife?

A month or two after he met Allegra, he brought her home for the weekend. This was new. A proper introduction.

"He's growing up," Jeb said.

"He texts with punctuation," Suzanne agreed.

They served dinner without gluten, then ice cream in elegant flavors. Jeb stirred his nervously until it began to melt, the colors running together into an ugly soup. He took out a spliff and offered it to Allegra. Her spoon was in her mouth. For a moment, Suzanne let herself imagine Allegra was going to say yes. Or else she would say no, but her refusal would be full of conviction. Maybe there was something secret about her—a hidden talent for making scenes.

Allegra swallowed, then declined politely. The spoon was clean when she set it down on the table. She went back to being thin-thighed and small-eared, the kind of girl Suzanne might once have hated or might once have been, she couldn't remember which. Allegra's bowl was still half full. Spencer gave her a reassuring look.

After dinner, he said he wanted to show Allegra around the high school.

"Spencer loved high school," Suzanne said disapprovingly, drizzling blue soap over a pile of plates in the sink.

"Spence was salutatorian." Jeb gave him a thump on the back.

"He had zero angst." Suzanne's hands disappeared beneath foam. "And zero acne."

"I want Allegra to smell the track," Spencer said. "What would be really great is if she could see the stadium lights turn on." He smiled, picturing it.

Allegra smiled back. "But it's okay. I've seen it in football movies."

When they left, Suzanne got the step stool from the basement so she could reach the liquor cabinet. She tugged at the hem of her shirt down when it revealed her stomach. The right glasses weren't where they should have been, so she poured the whiskey into champagne flutes. Jeb ducked his head sheepishly.

"No thanks."

"Oh, come on."

"I'll get a headache," he said while she drank the first glass in one efficient gulp.

She raised the second one in the air.

"To our son."

"Susie."

Later, bending down in the bathroom to charge her electric toothbrush, Suzanne heard Spencer and Allegra having sex on the other side of the wall. The bed frame creaked. The noise embarrassed her, as if the whole thing were a parody. There was no whispering or groaning, but she could hear the sucking and unsucking of skin, like feet in mud.

Suzanne decided to hire a new designer, even though there wasn't really room in the budget. Laird was thirty-seven and barrel-chested. He drank coffee in the evening and lost his cool on the phone with the cable company. He was astonishingly good at his job.

In the first months after she hired him, Suzanne walked purposefully around the block two or three times a day to talk herself out of her attraction. She told herself that it was predictable—mortifying. She looked at her reflection in the new chrome buildings while she walked: there was always something to dislike. This, too, was predictable. She saw another woman adjust her hair in a Starbucks window—hair made brittle by heat and dye and time—and hurried away in the opposite direction before her own image appeared in the glass.

There was a food court where people from nearby offices waited in long lines for custom-made salads. Suzanne liked to sit nearby and watch them. They were mostly young people, with wrinkled clothes and theatrical voices.

"I have a date with the girl from coat check," one woman told another.

Suzanne's table was covered in someone else's crumbs. She chewed a piece of gum until it lost its flavor, then sucked it.

"Would you like a crunch?" the man behind the salad bar asked the women.

They both ordered sunflower seeds and moved farther down the line.

"I'm keeping a Post-it with my phone number in my purse," the second woman said.

"Next time you'll be ready."

"Is that old-fashioned?"

"Protein?" the man said.

"Old-fashioned could be cute."

The man chopped their salads into pieces with a huge knife and Suzanne walked back to the office. Big gusts of wind blew her hair over her face, blinding her. While she walked, she recited all the phone numbers she knew by heart. The oldest ones were the easiest. Her sister, her sister-in-law. The neighbor in Berkeley with the extra key and the sourdough starter. Spencer's pediatrician. The numbers were useless now. Her phone knew them all.

Back at the office, Suzanne couldn't sit still. Her feet ached, so she took off her shoes. Plain leather boots, which would have disappointed a younger version of herself. The plainness was supposed to prove their expensiveness.

"My husband and I used to trim the calluses off each other's feet," she told the assistants, and she could see they were afraid to show their disgust. When Laird brought her a mug of hot water, she held it against her cheek, hoping that the wind had made her skin look pink and full of life.

There was a party at an old Italian restaurant to celebrate the firm's latest project. An alumni magazine for a college in Maine—redesigned, the editors said, to appeal to young donors. Kids who got rich from robotic vacuums, recyclable sneakers, cookies made out of meat. For weeks, Suzanne had been looking at pictures of wholesome undergraduates. Reading on lawns or clambering over rocks, smiling in front of the Atlantic. The ocean, she thought, looked grey and unfriendly.

The restaurant had leather booths and decanters made of thick glass. Recently, it had been decided that this old-school décor made the restaurant authentic—cool. For the first time, reservations were hard to come by. After appetizers were served, Suzanne went to the bathroom with outstretched hands, fingertips glistening with calamari grease. When she opened the door—it was unlocked, she would remind herself later—Laird was leaning against the sink, a house key underneath his left nostril.

"Fuck," he said.

"Fuck," she repeated, because her mind was blank.

He put the key away and looked at her steadily, waiting for her to decide what to do. On the other side of the door, the party sounded like every other party: utensils clinking, people laughing, conversations trying to stay alive. The faucet was dripping, and when he turned the knob to make it stop, everything on their side of the door was quiet. She didn't think he looked afraid.

She kissed him, they were kissing. She ran her greasy fingers through his hair and he ran his powdered fingers across her gums. The cocaine tasted metallic, like traces of vomit. When she unbuckled his pants and held him—warm and not quite hard—in her mouth, she wanted to push him to the very back of her throat, where there was spit and acid.

She didn't do that. She stood up after a few seconds, a few unimpressive thrusts. He pulled up his pants, she washed her hands, they went back to the party. She watched him get his coat, pulling a red scarf out of its sleeve. The scarf covered his mouth and half his nose, and then he was gone. At the table, Suzanne submerged a piece of bread in her glass of wine. She ate a whole basket that way, the bread purple and soggy and sticking between her teeth.

That was all that ever happened with Laird. He took a week of vacation unannounced and posted only one picture—a sunset with all the usual reds and golds. He could have been anywhere. Later, someone saw him throw his phone against the wall, but Suzanne let it go. She kept taking walks around the block, bought new shoes that were the same as the old shoes. He moved to Berlin without a job, and she assured him he could count on a positive recommendation whenever the time came.

Suzanne hired a woman in his place. Someone with a good degree, a quiet voice, a daughter in kindergarten. Suzanne would have disliked her if she'd had the energy. Spencer and Allegra moved in together. An apartment with wall-to-wall carpeting and rubber plants in the corners that didn't get enough light. By then, Suzanne had stopped searching for Laird. Most people were easy to keep track of: texts and tweets and things called stories, which weren't really stories at all. Laird didn't leave the same traces. Maybe he'd grown quiet, or tired. Maybe he was just private. She could have looked harder, but Suzanne didn't want to seem—even to herself—like she was trying too hard. Jeb friended all their nieces and nephews. He wanted to learn about hashtags.

Suzanne took an S.S.R.I. She researched rare illnesses with vague symptoms.

"Brain fog," she said one morning in the kitchen, scrolling through alarming search results.

"Mist," Jeb said. "Maybe it's just mist."

When people asked, Jeb said he was retired. *From what,* Suzanne wanted to say, but didn't. He was more energetic than ever. He went running barefoot and called recipes projects. He made curry powder with a mortar and pestle.

It was the end of February—a leap year—when the lawsuit was filed. There had been no snow that winter. Suzanne kept a thick coat and a thin coat in her office closet to accommodate the erratic temperatures.

Sexual harassment.

Spencer had just emailed her an edited version of his résumé.

Hostile work environment. Lewd comments.

What's the difference, Spencer wrote, *between passive and active voice?*

She took a walk in the wrong jacket. Sweat beaded behind her knees and underneath her breasts.

She went home early and googled Laird the way she used to. There were dozens of photos now. She scrolled until she found the sunset, then worked her way back up to the present. Mountaintops and cupcakes and a girl with a long orange ponytail. He posted a selfie when he'd been sober for six months and another when he'd been sober for twelve. He wore glasses, smiled widely. Eventually, he got a dog with two different-colored eyes.

Suzanne edited the résumé. Spencer got the job. Sometimes the weather matched her feelings, and on those days Suzanne was calm. When spring arrived, the sun wouldn't stop shining, so she left the firm before anything worse could happen. She hired a lawyer, who wrote a lot of expensive emails. She threw out all her old clothes—silk and linen and wool—and bought outfits with made-up materials.

"How much is the vortex?" Suzanne asked a salesperson.

She had become the kind of person who went to the mall.

"The Gore-Tex?"

Suzanne bought waterproof jackets and pants, but the rain never arrived. The jacket could be compressed into a tiny ball. Summer came, the hottest one on record. She sat on the front porch while Jeb read. These days, he read only massive books. It was a matter of principle: stories that required commitment. She sat with an unopened newspaper in her lap, glaring each time he turned a page.

"We can endure this," Jeb said when he reached the end of a chapter.

Suzanne didn't respond. She went inside to get more ice.

"We've endured so much more than this," he called after her.

No one understood why Laird had waited so long. They kept asking, *Why now.*

Suzanne couldn't know for sure. She wasn't allowed to see him or make any contact with him. He hadn't posted a picture of himself in weeks.

"Because it was time," she said, as if on his behalf.

Her lawyer was younger than she was. An untidy beard and a baggy grey suit. They tried to resolve everything over email, but in the end the mediators met in a building with dozens of identical conference rooms. Suzanne had to wait by herself in an empty room, where someone had left a pitcher of lukewarm water and no cups. When they took a break for lunch, her lawyer repeated it like a mantra: *why now, why now, why now.* Suzanne opened a clamshell container and lettuce went everywhere.

"It takes a while for things to sink in," she said.

The lawyer frowned. "Do you want me to win this or what?"

It felt like the most natural thing in the world to give Laird what he wanted. Suzanne pictured him somewhere else in the building, drinking straight from the plastic pitcher, water dribbling down his neck. She wore spandex and sneakers and wandered the hallways even though she'd been told not to. Jeb texted and she typed a reply, then erased it. All the other rooms on the floor were locked. After a few more hours, the lawyer came back and said everything was settled. He packed up his bag.

Up until the very end, Suzanne held out hope that Laird would appear. She waited while the elevator clanged up from the lobby, and when the doors opened, she was sure he would be inside. Long after the lawyer went home, she sat on a bench in front of the building, looking at everyone who walked by. She left her purse on the opposite end of the bench and wondered, vaguely, if it would be stolen. A bus pulled up to the curb but no one got off.

Suzanne imagined him running toward her, as if he'd been looking for her everywhere. He'd be shouting. He'd grab her wrist, or maybe her shoulders. He'd keep shouting, even when their faces were right in front of each other. Horrible, honest things, things he'd been meaning to say for years.

A security guard came out of the building and locked the door in two places.

"Everything all right?" he said when he saw her.

The man was younger than her, but he wasn't young.

"Everything's settled," she said.

He nodded sympathetically. She took the cigarette he offered her, like a kind of apology. When he'd walked away and she'd gathered up her purse, she said it again, just to herself: "Settled."

That night, she and Jeb sat on the porch again—sweating even once the sun went down. When she asked him for a divorce, he put his finger in the middle of a page so he wouldn't lose his place. He looked at her sadly and said okay.

Suzanne rented an apartment in a high-rise. The other tenants were people Spencer's age, with jobs in marketing or coding or search engine optimizing. There was a grill and a hammock in the shared courtyard. All the keys were cards.

"Stainless steel," Jeb said when he visited. "This isn't what a midlife crisis is supposed to look like."

"What were you expecting?" Suzanne bought plain white dishware and a TV with a complicated remote. "A compost bin? Too many pets?"

When Spencer was little, Jeb and Suzanne had owned a car that ran on vegetable oil. It couldn't drive very far or very fast and the fuel smelled like burning wax. Whenever they lit candles around the house Spencer said, *Vroom, vroom.*

As a housewarming gift, Jeb gave her a tiny succulent in a pot the size of a shot glass.

"The real danger is overwatering, not underwatering," he told her.

"No helicopter parenting."

Suzanne hesitated, looking for a place to put the plant, even though there was no shortage of available surfaces. End tables without lamps, bare bookshelves, too-clean counter-tops. She cupped the small pot in both hands, as if it were something to keep her warm.

Suzanne kept the plant alive and bought it company. Two cacti and a pot of ferns. Spencer and Allegra announced their engagement around the time her *Rebutia* was supposed to bloom but didn't. Suzanne worked on the wedding invitation while live-chatting with a horticulturalist. He recommended giving the plant a winter dormancy period. Store it someplace cool and dark.

Spencer called and asked her to come to the suit fitting. The wedding was still eight months away.

"Why?"

"Like, for moral support," he said. "To give compliments."

"Your dad is the one who can sew."

"Mom."

"Okay," she said.

The night before the fitting, Suzanne stayed up late making imperceptible changes to the invitations. She had forgotten this was the hardest part: deciding when to be done. She printed out three versions and looked at them for too long.

In the morning—she'd thought the decision might arrive in her dreams, or else in the shower—they were spread out on the table where she'd left them. From a distance, they were just blank squares. She knew what came next: she would stare at them again, from one angle, then another, in one order, then another. She would tell herself to concentrate. She would tell herself to choose. For now, she stood where she was, admiring the empty shapes.

TERMS OF AGREEMENT

•

There's a building under construction outside my window, close enough that when it's finished, there will be nothing but building in my line of sight. Progress has been slow and therefore mesmerizing. One morning, I watched two men assemble half a dozen floors of scaffolding. They were acrobats in metal-lined boots and many types of vests. The scaffolding came down recently, after so many months, and revealed a huge grey wall without a single window. The wall is what I'm looking at now—what I look at nearly all day long.

My first memory of you is sitting at the table in Nicole's kitchen, writing a story that was going to get you in trouble with your girlfriend. Later, you remembered this—the kitchen, the story, the girlfriend—but you didn't remember me being there.

I was just stopping by, because spontaneous visits were a kind of proof of loyalty to Nicole, especially when she was lonely—when she was in between girlfriends or in between shows. I don't think I ever took my coat off. One of the black puffy coats that everyone was wearing at the time, its puffiness and its ubiquity a precious insulation. I was skinnier than I should have been, and I was always cold.

You were sitting at your laptop, drinking straight from a gallon jug of water and tugging nervously at your beard. The story was for a class you were taking in the evenings, taught by a well-known writer. A writer with enviable success, a kind of fame that seemed to befit a different profession: people knew his name and his face, they got sentences from his books tattooed in visible places. There were a few political issues the writer had decided to care about, and when he spoke out about them he was treated, strangely, as an authority. Your girlfriend liked his novels more than you did, and she agreed with his political opinions.

That afternoon, you told me the story wasn't really fiction.

"Oh," I said, "one of those," and in my memory you smiled. You'd changed names, switched a few things around—the usual partial disguise. In the middle of the story, you'd copied and pasted an email from your girlfriend. At first, you'd intended to alter it in little ways, maybe even in meaningful ways. But then you kept writing, and it became impossible to dismantle.

"You can't improve the truth," I said, which I meant as another joke. You frowned.

The way I remember it there was silence, the three of us looking off into different vacant spaces. Eventually, Nicole took over. She told us a story about her friend the professional hockey player. All her stories were about her friend *the.* The hockey player, the speechwriter, the glass blower. (I wondered sometimes how I appeared in these stories, or whether I did, since I wasn't *the* anything. I had a nonspecific job, a vague creative ambition, a family that sounded interesting only if I told the right anecdotes.) The hockey player had been married for years, even though he was only twenty-five. He and his wife had known each other since they were kids. They were more in love, Nicole said, than anyone she'd ever met. And yet the wife had never attended a single one of his hockey games. It was a matter of principle. She'd seen a brawl on the ice once and had never gone back. The punching, the yelling, the hands made grotesque in their huge foam gloves. It was even worse when the fight was over. She could feel the satisfaction in the stadium, in the men on the ice and the men in the stands. It was the pleasure of spent energy, like a room after sex. Then the game went on as usual, except she couldn't stop thinking that on the bottom of every skate was a knife.

The two of you kept talking, eating from a large bowl of popcorn until it was the kernels you were eating. I could hear them crack between your teeth. Nicole went into the kitchen to refill the empty bowl and for a while you looked at your computer screen. There were a few stray pops from the stove. Without looking up, you said, "The story doesn't really matter."

It would be read by no more than twelve people, and only because they were required to. Your girlfriend would ask to read it, too, and there was no question that she would recognize her own words. You said she looked for herself in everything you wrote.

"Does she find herself?"

You nodded. "Even when she isn't there."

There was a crescendo of popping, faster and louder, and it seemed to me as though we were defying something by sitting still, by thinking and speaking slowly. And then the popping stopped.

"Maybe," you said, "the thing I'm most afraid of is that she won't be angry at all." Nicole appeared with the bowl. You grabbed a handful, then let it go, surprised by the heat. "That she might even be pleased."

I wanted to say something—the right thing. Instead, I left in my zipped-up coat, my tongue worrying the shard of a popcorn kernel in between my teeth. And it felt good—like the mortifying pain of a period cramp or a sudden spasm in the arch of my foot—that you looked up only briefly, that my departure was unremarkable, that I could be certain there was nothing I had left behind.

I've been looking for mailboxes lately, wondering if this is a letter I'll ever send. In my neighborhood, half of them have been painted green and padlocked. I guess they're empty, though sometimes I picture a stack of envelopes trapped inside, each one licked shut and Forever-stamped.

I was never a writer the way you and Nicole were. I never took classes or entered contests or learned to like the readings where everyone squinted while they listened, where every plastic cup was filled with half an inch of wine. I never sent out my work, which meant I never had it returned: the package addressed in my own handwriting, a form letter with no signature.

When I imagine all the things I've written, I imagine them piled up in the kitchen, the mess of an old woman who can't bear to part with her Tupperware—flimsy plastic in every imaginable size, because someday it might be just the thing she's looking for. The beginning of a story, the title of an essay. The journals, the text messages with lowercase *i*'s, the emails signed *yours* or *yrs*, the ones I've started signing *xx* because someone British started doing it first, someone who is at once forbidding and kind, one *x* blown into the ether and the other erected like a shield.

To find the nearest mailbox, I pass the construction workers on a break, sitting in whatever shade they can find, their legs stretched out across the sidewalk. In the morning, when I feel cool and light and younger than I really am, they are already sweating and eating lunch. Their helmets are empty bowls on the sidewalk; the hats underneath are white with their bodies' salt. They have earned their rest, their sandwiches in Saran Wrap, their huge containers of rice. And then there is nothing interesting in the words I have written and refused to throw out. I want muscles and a big appetite. I want to make a building and leave it outside someone else's window.

Three days a week, I'm a dog walker. The dog-walking company is owned by my neighbor, Konstantin. His best friends are successful entrepreneurs. Until recently, they all lived together, hatching ideas in the kitchen, vaping and tapping notes on their phones. The friends live in Manhattan now. They have it made, Konstantin says. I suspect this is an exaggeration, but I like the expression. Is there a difference: making it and having it made?

The dog-walking company is Konstantin's attempt at madeness, and I am in no position not to help. Most of my jobs—odd jobs, they used to be called—involve being alone in front of a computer, sending emails to people I will never meet. I proofread their résumés, correct typos in their letters To Whom It May Concern. A woman who signs every text *sincerely* pays me to Skype with her daughter—in college, a major she made up—whenever deadlines approach.

There were six or seven dogs at the beginning, but now there are only two. A pair of elderly Labradors in a studio apartment. *Roommates,* their owner says. They have grizzled white snouts and bad hips. They can hardly squat to take their shits. At least, Konstantin says, they have each other.

More than a year passes between my first memory of you and my second. Your girlfriend was gone by then. The famous writer had incurred the wrath of certain people online, which didn't stop him from writing books and didn't stop the tattoo-getters from reading them. The new books were less popular than the old ones, but he'd started dating a celebrity—a real one—and in this way his fame did not diminish.

We were at a party at the end of the summer, in the mosquito-infested backyard of someone Nicole had recently decided she loved. I arrived late, you arrived even later. Paper plates were being swept into a big trash bag, the embers in the grill had turned grey and dusty, and this belatedness seemed like a kind of intimacy. We stood next to a plastic bucket of beers that had once been filled with ice and now was filled with water, which was where we met Nicole's friend the evangelical. His name was Josiah.

He was the kind of evangelical who likes beer—also mushrooms and salvia; the celestial-feeling stuff, he said— and he plunged his hand into the bucket alongside ours. We stood there, our forearms dripping, while he explained that the reason God's love is better than everyone else's is that it's unconditional. There were, he admitted, human replicas that strove for the same steadfastness. Maternal love, say, and the kind of marital love that actually lasts. But it was only divine love that could really be said to have zero strings attached.

I slapped a mosquito and got blood on my hand. I told Josiah that sounded awful. I told him I wanted conditions—as many, preferably, as I could get.

"Why is being let off the hook a form of love?"

I told him—I didn't look at you—that I didn't want to be loved *in spite of*: my mood swings and my neck pain, my secret arrogance and my secret laziness, my bad dental hygiene and my leftovers molding at the back of the fridge.

Josiah was a little drunk already, and his evangelism made him seem drunker. He scraped the label off his beer bottle a little too vigorously. He rocked back and forth on his heels. He was in the middle of a sentence when a woman came up beside him, tugging on his arm the way a little kid might, saying something excitedly. His whole body came alive with her urgency, as if all this time he had been waiting for someone, maybe anyone, to arrive with that childlike command: *come look*. The commotion spread through the yard, and gradually all the remaining guests followed them inside.

We stayed where we were, the warm beer in the warm water in between us. In the silence, I cataloged the things I had revealed to you. My dark moods, my dirty teeth. With Josiah, they had been effortless to divulge, as if they were merely evidence in an argument, as if they didn't really have anything to do with me.

"Quite a character," I said.

"Yeah."

You shook your head, as if trying to shake your hair away from your face, but it was slicked to your forehead with sweat.

"I'm afraid one day I'll use him," you said, finishing your beer.

"Use him?"

"You know, it'll come up in conversation. Love, or faith. Or maybe it won't, and I'll just see a way to fill the silence."

"For the sake of a story," I said, and you nodded.

"Would it be so bad?" I asked. "Is he really so sacred?"

You put the empty bottle back in the water, where it bobbed on the surface.

"Maybe not." If we had been sitting down, our knees might have touched, or our shoulders. Standing up, the distance between us couldn't be bridged by accident. "Or maybe everyone is?"

And so we vowed that evening not to use Josiah. I haven't told anyone about him, but I think about him often. I wonder what will happen to him, or what already has. Eventually, he'll tell someone he loves them no matter what. In sickness and in health. Till death—or, I guess, beyond it. I wonder if together they will have agreed to total devotion, or if they will acknowledge the taut but not unbreakable strings that bind them, the promise they will always be making: to sway with the force of something unseen, to love and also to believe.

When the party was over, we met Nicole on the front steps.

"Oh good," she said, "you found each other."

This spoiled something for me, as if she had predicted whatever had transpired between us. Her hair was unbrushed and I remember the strap of her dress slipping down her shoulder. She made a point of always seeming a little undone. She told us that the commotion had been about a bird's nest wedged in the corner of the kitchen windowsill, twigs poking through the screen and into the rack of drying dishes. Inside the nest were three tiny birds, pink and unfeathered. A consensus had emerged that they were in danger of falling. The sill was narrow, the nest was lopsided. Everyone crowded around the sink, arguing among themselves about what to do, when suddenly a man in the group opened the window and pulled the nest inside. Nicole paused in her telling of the story. Her face fell, she sighed heavily.

"So that's the end of that," she said. You and I looked at each other uncertainly, and our puzzlement seemed to exasperate her.

"Everyone knows," she said, "that a bird won't come near her babies if they've received a human touch."

. . .

There is nothing stopping me from hand-delivering this letter. There were many mornings, years ago, when I walked from your house to mine. It was a long walk—there was a bus I might have taken—but I was trying to postpone my arrival, to let the feeling of being with you languish. Back then, this seemed to me like a necessary condition for being in love: to be immune to, or ignorant of, the waste of time. In fact, that was the last time I experienced it, though I have been in love since, as I hope you have, too. On one of those mornings, the sun burned the part in my hair, and for the rest of the day I was consumed by the image of my scalp, white and unknown, streaked with one perfectly straight pink line.

We fell in love and Nicole fell apart. Is that an unfair way to tell it? It had happened before, we knew that much, even though neither you nor I had been there. She had long since turned it into a story: coming undone. The story was unoriginal, and I was ashamed to realize that I held the generic details against her. Sleeping too much, eating too much, drinking too much. A grey cloud descending.

We were in a movie theater when Nicole called and wouldn't stop calling. It was October, but already turning cold, and I wore a new coat. Not warm, but elegant. The saddest film of the year, we'd been assured, which was the only kind I ever wanted to watch. I explained the catharsis of this to you—being hollowed out by something that had nothing to do with me. Sounds like a fun date, you said, smiling.

And so I was crying when I ignored Nicole's first call, and then the second. The third time, we went out into the lobby and I called her back. Everywhere we looked, the faces of famous actors stared out from posters. There were crumbs flattened into the carpet.

At Nicole's apartment, I went inside and you waited on the sidewalk, as she had instructed. I apologized too many times for this. You had known her so much longer. You'd met her dad, her sister, even one of her second cousins. You were the first one to read her first story. Together, you took mushrooms at the botanical garden, wondering at the alien armor of cacti, the secret language of tree bark. I couldn't even remember which floor she lived on.

Nicole was lying on a shaggy white rug. Her crying proved that I had never really cried. In her chest was what sounded like a broken motor, revving and wheezing. When she looked up at me, her face was liquid, snot shining on her chin. We lay there on the rug for a while. I said stupid things like *breathe,* and she nodded, still sputtering. Eventually, when there was quiet, she closed her eyes and gestured toward the next room. She had peed in her bed.

Nicole watched me strip sheets. The urine was a fierce and unexpected yellow.

"I'm always thirsty," she said. "But I can't get up."

The fitted sheet snapped into a heap.

"I just can't get up."

The naked mattress was mortifying. Sweat stains and bloodstains and long strands of hair. Grey specks of lint everywhere. I tried to think of something trivial to say, something distracting.

"Is what they say about dust true?" Nicole looked at me blankly. "You know, it's all just dead skin?"

As soon as the sheets were gone, she lay down again,

her face pressed into the pillow without its case. She looked up when my phone rang, and when she saw your name, her body curled in on itself, like a cat, or the kind of bug that can turn into a ball. No, she said. Or maybe she didn't have to. From the kitchen window, I could see you on the sidewalk, your phone between your ear and your shoulder, blowing into your hands for warmth. When the buzzing in my hand stopped, you looked up, but the lights were off and you couldn't see me. You stood like that, your face tilted up, as if basking in the streetlamp's glow, and then you turned and walked away.

Nicole kept detergent in a quart milk container. The man who owned the Laundromat lent me a cap for measuring. I watched the other customers absorbed in their tasks, peeling socks away from shirts, shaking polyester until it let its static go. I tried to follow the same navy blue something as it whirled inside one of the machines, but I lost track of it right away, my blue blurring into all the others.

The day after Thanksgiving, Nicole checked herself into the hospital. She stayed for more than three weeks, until Christmas Eve. In those weeks of waiting, the city turned ugly to me—all its seasonal rituals cold and meaningless. Snow fell overnight and was grey by noon. The subways were crowded with shopping bags, dripping boots and dripping noses. In the morning, Christmas lights were just green plastic wires, strangling every arm of a tree.

We visited twice a week, with clean clothes and snacks. The nurse reminded us of the rules each time: laceless shoes, zipperless coats, no visitors after six, no calls after nine. Half of the time, Nicole declined to see us.

When she checked herself out, Nicole didn't call you until she was at the airport. That night there were carolers in the park across from my apartment. I could hear you on the phone in the hallway; I could see the candles cupped in their hands. She was flying across the country. She said this as if it were the most normal thing in the world. *Home for the holidays.*

You refused to be angry.

"You're allowed—" I said, and you cut me off with one look.

In the morning, we drove north to your parents' house, at the end of a potholed road, with a view of nothing but trees. Everything went right that trip: four feet of snow and something always in the oven. But you were quiet and distracted—the smoke detector reminded you there were cookies baking—and I surprised myself by filling the space that you had withdrawn from. I was a new audience for traditions that were getting old. I'd never decorated a Christmas tree, couldn't believe eggnog was really made out of eggs. Everyone was grateful for me, without quite knowing why. Someone's dog lunged at someone's niece and I swept her up in my arms, just in time.

When we got back, the day after the first day of the year, Nicole had so much to tell us. She was writing poetry. A TV pilot, too. She was done with doctors. She was dating a curator. She was better. She wanted us to pretend nothing had ever happened.

For months, every time we saw her—we kept seeing her,

we kept worrying about her—the first thing she did was tell us about her latest change. She painted her bedroom walls, then her bedroom floor. She lasered the hair in her armpits, pierced her tragus, asked her dentist to remove all her fillings. There were so many people, she told us, carrying mercury in their mouths. I wasn't sure any of this made her happy—her ear swelled and oozed—but telling us about it did.

When her sister's wedding invitation arrived in the mail, Nicole insisted we attend.

"You'll be my dates," she said, wrapping one arm around each of our shoulders. The curator was already gone, hardly missed.

The wedding took place at a summer camp. It was the beginning of June and the cabins were empty, but we found a raincoat and a vibrator in the bunk room where the guests slept, which was how everyone started talking about teenage romance. We all wanted to remember it—the special thrill of what we'd called summer love, the hot months in which it had seemed we were sweating away one self, becoming another.

When it was Nicole's turn, she told the story of kissing a girl for the first time. It had seemed like magic while it was happening.

"Magic," she repeated. "I know it sounds dramatic."

But that's what it was. Late at night, on a dock, when the water and the sky were the same unmoving black. Their lips touched and then their chests—not breasts really, not yet—and Nicole could have sworn she heard the sound of a fish leaping in the air.

And then in the morning the magic was gone. Just like

that. The flag on the flagpole was limp, the oatmeal at break-fast was congealed. The girl sought out Nicole's foot under the table and it wasn't thrilling; it was clumsy, unbearable. Everywhere she turned, this ordinariness was an accusation. What have you done?

That night there was a dance. Nothing special: acoustic guitars and chaperones. Nicole found the tallest boy and pulled him into the center of the crowd. They kissed under a cheap disco ball. His tongue was muscular and wet. She closed her eyes and her head throbbed with what might have been pain, a vague heat that was easy enough to pretend was desire.

She ignored the girl for the rest of the summer. On the last day, everyone gathered on the hill that led down to the lake, hugging and crying and vowing to stay in touch. Nicole saw the girl looking for her, craning her neck in the crowd. She let the girl find her. She let their eyes meet for a second, just long enough to be sure that they were dull, desperate eyes, and then Nicole turned away. They never spoke again. A dozen years went by, and then the girl—a woman now, like us—opened a restaurant in Nicole's neighborhood. Her name appeared in the newspaper, a rave review. The restaurant served food with "feminine energy." There was a pink sign out front, the name of a goddess in neon script. Nicole told us it was impossible to avoid. Every time she passed by, she crossed the street. Through the window, she saw the waiters' harried grace, the tables crowded with plates and elbows, the laughter that seemed all the more ecstatic because she couldn't hear it. Once, Nicole thought she saw the woman—hair pulled back, her hands doing something deftly above a frying pan—and the old shame clenched inside her. She was sweating, or else shivering. Either way, she was trapped, her new self immobilized inside her past self. Like a bug, she said, in amber.

Some of Nicole's friends insisted she should face her fears. Make a reservation, introduce herself, leave a generous tip. Right the wrongs.

"But I can't," she said. "She might never let me forget."

The other wedding guests nodded.

"That's how I feel about my mother," one of them said, and the laughing resumed.

I smiled a fake smile because I didn't believe Nicole. She had told other, more outrageous lies, but their implausibility had never bothered me before: they were good stories. And yet this one seemed invented just for me.

"But it doesn't have anything to do with you," you said when I told you.

"Of course it does." I pictured the amber before it was amber, when it was just sap, dripping or flowing or moving too slow to be seen.

It was a story Nicole knew I would see through. She and I had been to that restaurant one afternoon in the spring. It was raining, the piles of pear blossoms along the sides of the street a soggy beige mass. Inside, the tables were all empty, and the owner served us herself. She was probably in her fifties, the sort of middle-aged woman who didn't make an effort to seem younger than she was: undyed hair and a plain, leathery face. We drank tea from individual-size pots, and when we left, I said to Nicole, *Do you think we'll grow up like that?*

The wedding ceremony was about to begin. We took our seats in the last row, with the guests who had brought their babies or forgotten their ties. The music started. We stood up and sat down as instructed. A velvet bag of rings was passed down the rows, so that it could be warmed by all our hands. I held the bag too long, tracing each ring through the fabric, listening for the slight scrape of metal on metal. You had to take it out of my hands.

Nicole found us after the toasts, her eyes glistening. Her cheeks, too.

"Tears of joy," she said, with a note of pride. Her dress was darkened with sweat.

"Do those really exist?" I asked.

You glared at me, and Nicole ignored us. She was smiling, tugging us toward the dance floor. I did what she told us to, even though my feet were heavy and my wine spilled and my clothes would need dry cleaning. You danced away from me, spun Nicole's teenage cousin around and around in circles, her head tipped back, her face frozen with the thrill of almost letting go. When it was all over, when I was lying on the top bunk, imagining that I could feel you staring up from the bottom bunk, then worrying that I couldn't—feeling, instead, the empty chill of your closed eyes—I said it to myself again and again: it has nothing to do with you.

If I could choose the story of how I found out about Nicole's book, it would appear for the first time behind the glass of a bookstore's display window. I would stop in the mid-

dle of a bustling sidewalk, like a rock interrupting the stream.
Then the book and I would be two objects.

Instead, I found out about it online. It was the middle of
the night and all the windows had turned into mirrors. On
the website where I bought the book, there was a picture
of the cover, a blue background with blocky, old-fashioned
letters. When I hovered my cursor over the image, an invitation appeared: *see inside!* It seemed like a dare, or a taunt,
so I didn't click. I didn't look for her photo, but I imagined
it, her head tilted the way authors' heads always are, the
background blurred into something indistinct but elegant. I
turned off all the lights and lay there not sleeping, the laptop
faintly humming beside me, waiting for the sun to come up,
for the construction workers to arrive.

I read the book twice. First in bed and all at once, and
then again in the world, in snatches of pages, not caring
where I started or finished. (I remember being interrupted
while reading as a child: *just let me get to a good place.*) I
read it on the train and on a bench with the two Labradors
breathing damply on my legs. I read it in a park surrounded
by a squadron of empty strollers and at another park observed
by elderly tai chi practitioners. I let strangers read over my
shoulder. I left it, briefly, at the Laundromat, and when I
went back and found it on top of the rumbling dryer, the
dust jacket was warm with the machine's heat.

We're not the only ones in Nicole's book. The hockey
player and the hockey player's wife, or ex-wife. Half a dozen
of her girlfriends: the model, the piano tuner, the disgraced
politician's daughter. Two or three Christians, so it's a little

hard to figure out who's who. There's her friend who got me
my first real job, who turned out to be sleeping with my first
real boss. Nicole's brother, the one with a farm, and Nicole's
other brother, the one with a car that drives itself. She has not
changed names so much as shuffled them. Mine has been
reassigned to the nurse at the psychiatric unit, who confis-
cated Nicole's notebook and fountain pen and box of a hundred paper clips. She is neither the good nurse nor the bad
nurse, so I can't tell whether to be offended. She disappears
after a few pages. Nicole's father is called Josiah. His own
name is given to a teenage patient who slits his wrists: Bob.

You are the only one who remains unchanged. Your
name is your name.

For a long time, I wasn't sure what this made me feel.
Your name, over and over again. Your name and your beard,
your name and your sneakers, the ones you've always worn,
your name and your thin gold bracelet, the one you started
wearing right before I never saw you again. Your name and
the things you said. The things you said to me. The things
you said to Nicole you'd said to me.

I considered that I might be angry, and for a while I was
sad. But above all I was envious. Not envious that Nicole
had known you better. I had long since accepted that the
intimacy between you and me would be eclipsed, that love
is only ever singular in the details—the popcorn, the bird's
nest—never in intensity, rarely even in longevity. What I am
really envious of is that she captured you.

I have never been especially interested in writing stories like Nicole's, but I've tried it here and there, plucking

people and things out of life and putting them down on the page. For the most part, it isn't too hard. It's a kind of guilty pleasure, to see how efficiently one person can take shape: the slope of a nose, the shriek of a laugh, the joke they won't stop telling, the boyfriend they bring everywhere. But with you it's impossible. Hundreds of times I have tried to write what you look like, to remember exactly the words you said, and because it isn't perfect it's all wrong. I have sat for hours thinking of what name to give you instead of your real name—your name is common, anything would do, nothing would—and never once did it occur to me to simply keep it the same.

Was the book a success? I never checked, though not because I wasn't curious. That kind of envy is so much smaller, so much less frightening.

We broke up a few weeks after the wedding. Nicole had been admitted to an important writing program, and we went to the celebrations in her honor—too many of them, everyone eager to make her good fortune official, to prove that whatever had come before it was an aberration, a wheel briefly skidding off the road. We rode the subway to the last party in silence. There was a stroller in the aisle in front of you, and the baby kept trying to meet your gaze—a coy, precocious smile. You didn't notice, so I elbowed you, but it was too late. The baby had looked away. The party was at a bar with a fireplace. The summer was in full swing, and the logs were untouched and somehow ominous. Nicole's sister was there—married, pregnant, though we didn't know it then—

and Nicole leaned in to her, bickering pleasantly over the bill. Someone grabbed it out of their hands, insisting.

You and I walked home, even though it was a long walk. You said you couldn't bear to go back underground. Did we already know what was happening? We took the bridge, but we didn't stop in the middle, halfway between the islands, above the loud cars and the dark water, because that would have been too symbolic. We said goodbye on the other side, in a park where the trash cans overflowed and the trees were heavy with leaves. We kissed and apologized and clutched futilely at each other's clothes. I didn't tell you that Nicole and I had found ourselves in the restaurant bathroom, looking at each other in the unclean mirror, that she said how sorry she was that you hadn't been admitted to the program. How much you deserved it, how sure she was that one day it would all work out for you.

I didn't ask why you hadn't told me. I watched you walk away and let myself imagine that you were resisting the urge to turn around.

I never saw you again, although I bumped into Nicole a few times before she left the city. We always said we'd get coffee, and I'm surprised that I can't remember if we ever actually did.

In the middle of the book, Nicole and I stand side by side at bathroom sinks. I know it's me, although my name is the name of a girl I met once or twice, at a dinner party or someone's birthday in the park. Nicole doesn't speak. The only sound is the automatic soap, the hand dryer that won't stop drying. I have avoided her eyes all night, but now, in the mirror, I look.

I can remember the smell of the hospital—like an airplane, plus dry-erase markers—and the sound of the nurses' sneakers on the just-mopped linoleum. I can remember the worn-white spines of detective novels in what was called the library, which was just a few bookshelves. I can remember the sticky cartons of juice and packages of shortbread cookies. I can remember the afternoon I brought a five-pound bag of sunflower seeds, because the brand's motto was: *Eat. Spit. Be happy.* I can remember that Nicole was helpless, and I was not enough help.

In everything I've written, you are only ever there in pieces, or in flashes. (Am I putting you there or finding you there?) The softness of your voice, the softness of your hair. The time we stole a peach from the bins in front of the supermarket, just because we'd always been tempted. The only time you cried. You cried and cried; you lay on the floor and I lay on your back and our bodies heaved up and down until, little by little, they didn't.

I imagine one day I'll read Nicole's book again. By then, I won't know where you live and won't have a way of finding out. Even if I did: will mailboxes still exist? By then, I'll be remembering remembering. Two characters will stand in front of a mirror in silence, and I—a person who does not yet exist, a person I have yet to invent—will wonder anew at all that is left unsaid.

Anew. It's a small form of alchemy. It's worth waiting for. Like building a building, like finding God, like getting old and stacking Tupperware and wishing for your life, at last, to be contained.

OBJECTS OF DESIRE

•

The two of them live in a small apartment, small enough that it is impossible to ever be truly out of sight. In the room that is both the living room and the bedroom, there is a lofted bed. They have learned, faster than they anticipated, to navigate the ladder in half-sleep, when one of them needs to pee or retrieve a glass of water or confiscate the cat's rubber toy, which squeaks each time it's chewed. Lately, they wonder if having the cat in such a small space is ethical. Unlike the apartment, the first important thing they have shared, the cat is Jon's and has been for many years: since the days when he did not expect, or perhaps even want, other companionship.

This was a private and intense time in his life—a dark time, or at least a dim time, but the kind of dimness that can be soothing in its muted constancy. Now that it's over, it has also become, in its way, a sacred time. Leonora does not believe in this sacredness, but she understands why it's useful to Jon and takes care not to violate it. To become truly happy, she tells one of her friends, is to betray the unhappy person you used to be. The friend disagrees. No, the friend says, it is to liberate that person.

Leonora is cautious around the cat. He is named Buddy, which Jon thinks is unfairly considered a dog name. If, when Leonora comes home at the end of the day, Buddy is curled up in Jon's lap, she does her best not to startle them, speaking quietly and gently—out of something like respect.

The man Leonora once believed she would marry, Julian, has recently become something of a political sensation. A few weeks ago, he was elected to Congress. His district is across the country, on the opposite coast. Julian's victory surprised many people, and this surprise has produced nationwide fame. He is known for his youth, his charm, and his refusal to wear a tie. His clothing is taken as a sign of sincerity. Several commentators observe that the Pope, a radical man, also dresses casually—humbly. Leonora happens to know that Julian is self-conscious about the thickness of his neck, which the knot of a tie can seem to accentuate. (He is, as many have noted, exceptionally handsome. In reality, his neck is a nice neck.) It will be a month before Julian is sworn in to Congress. For now, he tweets messages of thanks and hope, and appears on late-night TV.

On Election Day, Leonora and Jon had not spoken of Julian for many months. Early on in their relationship, he came up often, and always painfully. Leonora and Julian never lived together, but there were other things that made their love for each other seem fierce and true and somehow inviolable. They had exchanged love letters and endured a few pregnancy scares. Once, they had been accosted at knifepoint. They had gone to funerals together. Most of all, they had fought passionately.

Leonora and Jon speak kindly and judiciously when problems arise. They have never written each other letters; when they met, they were both relieved to agree that even text messages were distracting and prone to miscommunication. Pregnancy has never been a possibility, much less a fear. In the current political climate, Leonora, like many of her friends, decided the wisest thing was to get an I.U.D.

When the exit polls started coming in and it became clear that Julian would win—by a landslide, the headlines said—Leonora was sitting at the desk underneath the bed. Jon was above her, meditating. She waited for the gentle chimes on his phone to indicate that he was finished and then she said, without emerging from under the bed, "Julian won the race."

Several seconds passed, and then Jon's face appeared over the railing.

"Are you glad?" he asked.

He looked concerned, which irritated Leonora more than it should have. When Jon is concerned, his expression is always the same. His forehead slackens, his eyes look deeper than normal. It is an open and profound expression, and in times of great need, many people have been moved by it. On lesser occasions—in times of small need—Leonora is exasperated by it.

"Of course," Leonora said. "Julian has excellent politics."

At the same time, a friend texted her. In general, Leonora's friends believe she has been too tolerant of Julian's failings. Now that the relationship is over, they encourage her to criticize him. His ego, they tell her, is large and getting larger. This doesn't make Leonora immediately angry, but she wants to please them. The more passionate her displays of anger, the more gratified her friends are. *Admirable politically and abhorrent personally,* one of them likes to say about Julian—visibly pleased with this formulation. The same friend, Leonora notices, responds enthusiastically on Julian's private Facebook—the one without his last name, where he posts vacation photos and songs he likes.

"Right," Jon said. His forehead furrowed for a moment, and he touched it reflexively, as if to smooth it into serenity. From the corner, Buddy's rubber mouse squeaked. Jon looked at the cat and Leonora looked down at her phone, where two more friends had texted. They wanted her reaction. She wrote something funny and a little unkind, then copied it to all three friends.

In the first week of December, Jon's band plays a show in a concert hall made to look like a warehouse, because the fans love warehouses. The people in the audience are five or ten years younger than the people in the band. Backstage, there's a case of bad beer and a plastic tray of raw, dried-out vegetables. The baby carrots are more white than orange. Jon dips one into a pool of ranch dressing. The lead singer drinks a shot of ginger and chases it with beer. The other singer—the only woman in the band—applies pink eye shadow and nibbles, birdlike, on a bar of fancy chocolate.

"Ranch is very retro," she says, to no one in particular.

Leonora declines a celery stick and takes a walk through the assembling crowd. She waits in a long line for the bathroom, even though there's a smaller, cleaner one backstage, in hopes of eavesdropping on interesting conversation. The girls in front of her tilt their phones toward each other, scrolling and laughing conspiratorially, saying nothing. The boy behind her sucks silently on a black vape pen. When he exhales, it smells like fruit, or ChapStick. Leonora abandons the line.

"Your fans are all vaping," she says to the lead singer.

"Yeah," he says. "They're the future."

"You mean, they're kids."

He ignores her, licking ranch off his paper plate. Unlike Jon, who hunches over his guitar during shows, disappearing behind his limp hair, the lead singer is the face of the band. The face is not obviously handsome, but its features are sharp. He is often glaring, which makes them even sharper. At one point, the name of the band was his name.

"Are cigarettes uncool now?" Leonora asks.

She starts and stops smoking every winter. As soon as the temperature drops and seeing her own breath seems like a mean joke—a charade of substance, mocking her. Once, she had tried to explain the habit to Julian. I want to actually expel something, she said. I *think* I want, she added. Julian had smiled, as if this idea were one he had entertained briefly and long since outgrown, like a taste for sugary cereal, or overcooked meat, which betrays none of its slippery animalness. Now this mortifies her: not the thought itself—she still thinks it—but having said it out loud.

"Cigarettes aren't uncool," the lead singer says, "but they aren't new."

"I liked old things when I was a kid."

As a teenager, she had collected records and stamps and books with pages that crumbled into fine yellow dust if you turned them too quickly. Late at night, when the house was asleep, she had sipped shoplifted bourbon, because it smelled the way she imagined grandfathers did.

"They're not *kids*," Jon says, examining a piece of raw broccoli intently, as if uncertain how to go about eating it.

"Like, nostalgia for things I hadn't lost," Leonora continues. "Because loss seemed adult."

The female singer does a short line of coke and eats another square of chocolate. They are summoned onstage. Jon gives Leonora's shoulder a little squeeze before following the drummer through the door. She lingers in the room for a few minutes, surveying the vegetables and the drugs, listening to the muffled sounds of the first song. Eventually, she makes her way into the crowd. The music is unbearably loud. She can feel it inside her body, as if this is where it had originated all along, where it is desperate—pounding—to escape. She stands next to a boy and a girl locked in an embrace. Sweat forms in fat drops on their arms. The girl's ponytail looks wet. The songs crest and diminish and crest all over again, big waves of ecstasy that might have moved her, except that they exhaust her—an unwilling body, tossed around in noisy surf. The boy and the girl sway with the music, sometimes opening their eyes and sometimes closing them. During the chorus, they claw each other frantically, as if one of them is about to be snatched away.

"He doesn't seem like a rock star."

Leonora walks across the Brooklyn Bridge with her friend, a professor. A man on a bike speeds past, music blaring from a speaker strapped to his backpack.

"Rock star?" Leonora says. "Nobody says *rock star* anymore."

The friend would like to be a professor of Victorian literature, where she says all the wildest passions have been secreted away, but in reality she teaches whatever English classes are available. She complains that her students expect everything to be on the surface; they don't dig into the text.

"What I'm saying is that Jon is very understated."

"You love understated things."

"I didn't say I didn't love him."

They stop in the middle of the bridge. The sun reflects off the tall buildings on either side of the river, turning them solid white with light.

"Have you ever made a crowd go wild?" Leonora asks.

Her friend laughs. She has a pleasant laugh that puts people at ease, but her face is prettier when she is serious. To Leonora, this seems like an injustice—that joy does not automatically create beauty.

"With my lectures about *Middlemarch*?"

The shadow of a plane appears on the river, but Leonora doesn't look up.

"What do you think it feels like?"

They listen while the sound of the plane's engine fades away.

"Sometimes my classes are one hundred percent women," the friend says. "Skinny girls who email three times to confirm deadlines. They're smart, but mostly they're tired."

"Don't," Leonora says.

"Don't what?"

"Don't say something like, they just need to relax."

They begin walking again. The sun slips behind a skyscraper, and Leonora feels her eyes widen, though she had not been aware of them narrowing.

"Every couple of semesters, a boy registers. It might be an accident, or a joke." The friend grimaces. "And the horrible thing, but the true thing, is that those are the best classes. Suddenly everyone performs."

Another man bikes past. He wears a cycling jersey and shorts that cling to his thighs, hunched over as if he is part of some invisible race.

"The girls start writing better papers. They start washing their hair more."

"Does it matter if the boy is attractive?"

"They even start interrupting each other!"

They reach the end of the bridge. Buildings loom above them now. A tour group has assembled nearby, matching blue T-shirts visible here and there beneath sweaters and unzipped coats. A woman stands on a bench in front of them, brandishing a blue flag and speaking energetically in a language Leonora doesn't recognize. Her face makes big, eager expressions. Leonora looks away, embarrassed by the nakedness of her enthusiasm.

"The boys themselves have mediocre ideas."

"When are you supposed to stop calling them *boys*?"

"This year I took it a step further," the friend says in a confessional voice. "I went to the dean and I requested a boy. I said, any boy will do."

"I guess it's more important to stop calling them *girls*."

The tour guide finishes her speech. She raises her flag high in the air, and when she lowers it, she points it directly at Leonora. The tourists turn, staring. The flag seems accusatory. Leonora isn't sure what to do, so she stares back.

"The dean looked at me as if he'd won something, as if it were a victory."

A couple in the group bend their heads toward each other. One of them whispers something, the other one smiles a secret smile.

"And for you?" Leonora looks at her feet. "Did it feel like defeat?"

"Of course."

Abruptly, the tour guide climbs down from the bench. The group begins moving again, shuffling slowly as a single organism. They don't look back. For a few minutes, Leonora and her friend sit down on the vacated bench. The wind coming off the water is sharp against their unscarved necks. Her friend rolls each of them a cigarette, and they smoke quietly. Leonora finds a strand of tobacco on her tongue. She imagines it inside her body, and then she imagines many of them inside her body—like worms, wriggling past her crowded organs. She feels unclean, but solid. When she says goodbye to her friend, Leonora is glad to be rid of her, glad to be alone.

There are only a few weeks left in the year. The rest of Jon's band goes to California, where there is more space and more sun, where nobody worries about noise complaints and garage bands actually exist. Leonora encourages him to join them. Jon takes this encouragement to mean she is indifferent to his company—possibly even eager to be free of it. Leonora denies this. If it were her, she explains, she would go.

"If I had the chance," she adds.

Leonora's voice turns bitter when she says this. She is getting dressed for work, zipping up a skirt that is cheap and ugly, that leaves a red line across her waist at the end of the day. There are many aphorisms she isn't willing to say out loud. *Seize the day,* she could have said to Jon. *Live life to the fullest.* Leonora does not endorse these worldviews, but ingratitude makes her impatient, and unkind. In California, she thinks, she could drive with the windows open. She bends down to put on her boots, the soles white with chemical salt. She never gets a seat on the subway. By the time she arrives at the office—there are unsalted, uncomfortable heels waiting under her desk—her feet already ache.

"It's been months," she says, "since I drove a car."

Leonora's explanation only wounds Jon further: she does not care if he stays, and she herself longs to escape.

She can tell he is sleeping poorly. Several times, she wakes up in the middle of the night and he is sitting against the wall, staring at the mounds of his knees beneath the blankets.

One morning, Jon announces he is planning to attend a march. They have become accustomed to small protests organized and advertised on various social media platforms. This one is expected to be large. There are several others planned in cities across the country at the same time. Leonora is at the office when the march begins, and she's still there when it ends. Once or twice, she thinks she hears chanting from the street below, but the windows are soundproof. She texts Jon that she's glad he went. The implication is: *on our behalf.*

He finds more marches. Big ones she's heard about and small ones she hasn't. He stands in front of a congressman's office. Later, in front of a congressman's house. John tells Leonora these are called actions. He gathers in densely packed squares and stops traffic on wide avenues. He comes home with sore feet and signs other people made—slogans she has never heard him speak.

When Leonora asks if the band has been rehearsing in California, Jon comes close to getting angry. He retreats to bed, even though they've just finished dinner. Buddy stops licking his front legs while Jon climbs the ladder. Leonora washes the dishes and Jon pretends not to watch. The water is warm and soothing on her hands. She arranges the items in the drying rack carefully, to fit as many as possible. A ceramic bowl perches precariously, but doesn't fall. Jon's face is to the wall, so she goes up and lies down beside him.

For a few moments, she stays on her back, and the unnatural fact of the ceiling above her, close enough to reach out and touch, fills her with panic. When she is calm again, she turns and wraps her arms around Jon, pressing her chest against his back.

"I shouldn't have made you do the dishes," he says.

"You didn't make me."

"The guitar is frightening me."

"Okay."

"When I play, people don't hear what I hear."

He has explained this before. Leonora can't remember the exact details: it has something to do with sound waves, or with the special molds he wears in his ears during shows.

"It's like that for everyone," she says, reassuringly. "Does anyone really know the sound of their voice?"

"That's not what I mean."

Buddy scratches the wooden ladder, which might be a message, or might be a habit. In general, he isn't a plaintive audience.

"The ear is too close to the mouth, right?" Leonora rolls away from him and looks over the railing at the cat. "The sound can't be trusted at that distance."

"That's not what I mean."

Buddy continues scratching. Fine white lines in the yellow wood. As defacement goes, Leonora thinks, it's rather elegant.

"Stop it," Jon says suddenly—sharply—still facing the wall.

She is taken aback when Buddy looks up and meets her eye.

. . .

Leonora's boss sits a few feet away from her desk, behind a thick glass door that requires two hands to slide open. After lunch, he knocks on the glass to get her attention. She is in the middle of writing an email to his teenage children about their upcoming vacation. They go to the same island every year, but all they've ever really seen is the hotel. She writes the email from her boss's personal account and signs it *Dad*. He knocks again.

The boss has six sheets of paper arranged on his desk. On each piece of paper is a single tweet.

"This is the last straw," he tells Leonora.

The woman who has been tweeting works down the hall, in a cubicle with a stack of mugs stained coffee brown and lipstick red. Kelly is young, but no longer young enough to be considered promising. Her job is boring and essential. She lives alone, which Leonora knows isn't pitiful—it might be relaxing, even liberating—but sometimes, watching her brush her teeth at the bathroom sink or nibble on the pink-grey end of her pencil, it is. The tweeting started nine months ago. The symbolism is not lost on Leonora. What has she been gestating?

It was innocent enough, at first. Lions befriending birds, quotes from Rumi, selfies in mirrors. She made friends. Eventually, she found trolls—but who didn't? When Kelly first began complaining, her grievances were small, relatable. She hated winter. Summer, too. Airplanes were over-air-conditioned. Her office, too. There were a few jokes among coworkers—someone get Kelly a cardigan—and for a day or two Leonora thought the tweets might even be a good thing. A morale boost, a shot of team spirit. The office *was* cold. But Kelly didn't stop there. Did you know, she tweeted, that men and women have different optimal temperatures? That men wear collars and jackets while women suffer? The better you dress—strappy shoes, cute necklines—the colder you are. Workplace misogyny, she wrote.

One morning, dozens of likes became hundreds, which became thousands. Leonora watched the numbers tick up, second by second. She tried to visualize the crowds behind the numbers—a bus full, a room full, a stadium full—but it was like trying to picture big sums of money in piles of dollar bills. She couldn't keep track. There was a meeting with Kelly's boss, and for a little while the tweets turned mild again. A picture of her niece covered in pink yogurt traveled fast, but not too fast.

Within a few days, it was back: the exclamation points, the hashtags, the strangers clamoring for more. Her company, Kelly wrote, was run by patriarchs. She called them *moneybags, meat necks.* She alluded to private planes. She didn't name names, but she didn't really have to—her job was right there in her profile, underneath the photo of her and two curly-haired white dogs. In the middle of the night, she tweeted that she had reason to believe the gender pay gap was alive and well. The likes came in from London.

Leonora and her boss stand silently with the tweets between them. Enlarged, the font is pixelated—absurd. Her boss has big, fleshy earlobes, which he pulls when he's upset.

"Enough is enough," he says. "You'll have to tell her."

"What?"

"Enough, I said—"

"Me?"

He lets go of his ears.

"She can't stay." He sits down in his chair, a huge, ergonomic thing—black padded armrests, a leathery cushion for the back of his head—which reminds Leonora of a gorilla.

"Because of the tweets?"

"Keep it general, like a divorce. Irreconcilable differences."

"You want me to fire her?"

"Never say *fire*." He leans back in the chair and sighs heavily, an exhale meant to convey the weight of being powerful.

"What do I say? *Let go?*"

Leonora's phone lights up with an email from one of the kids. *Dibs on the king bed.*

"You just say, *Best of luck.*"

She and Kelly meet in a conference room, because neither of them has an office. In the center of the table, there are bottles of fancy sparkling water, which Leonora has never dared to try.

Kelly doesn't cry or rage, doesn't say much at all. Leonora is startled to remember that it has been months since they spoke in person. Kelly is quiet in the office, sputtering apologies at the copy machine, avoiding eye contact at the bathroom sinks. There is an awkward pause while Leonora wonders what else there is to say.

"You're a whole different person online," she says at last.

Kelly shrugs. "Not really."

"Don't you want them to know *this* person?" Leonora

points at Kelly, then realizes she's pointing, and drops her hand, embarrassed.

Kelly opens her mouth to speak, then starts coughing. Leonora looks away—is this the polite thing to do?—but the coughing doesn't stop. Kelly's face turns blotchy pink. When she reaches for a water, she looks at Leonora, as if for permission. The look fills Leonora with shame.

"Oh God. Of course." She does a wavy thing with her hand that means something like, *Help yourself.*

The bottles are made of dark blue glass and arranged in a triangle, like billiard balls. Kelly takes the one at the very top and gulps deeply. Eventually, the coughing stops, but Leonora can't help glancing at the ruined triangle.

"Have you noticed," she says, "that whenever one of the bottles disappears, it's always been mysteriously replaced by the morning?"

Kelly's face has returned to its normal color. She looks confused.

"Why is that a mystery?" Her voice, for the first time, has an edge. The bottle looks elegant in her hand. "It's just somebody's job."

The day before Leonora's boss leaves on vacation, he keeps asking her to check the weather on the island. The answer never changes. Six days of cheerful yellow suns; a seventh with a cloud but no rain. Outside the nearest window— Leonora reminds herself it is a privilege to be so close to her boss's window—it has been snowing on and off all morning.

Through the glass door, she sees her boss pick up the phone on his desk at the same time that the phone in her pocket starts vibrating. This is disorienting, and for a few seconds she is immobilized by her confusion. When she picks up, a stranger with a frantic, high-pitched voice explains that Jon has been arrested. The woman says Jon's name with affection and desperation. There's a loud noise, followed by many muffled noises. The phone being fumbled, then dropped. For several seconds, there is silence, which makes it feel to Leonora that she is literally inside the phone. She is the thing that has been overturned on the sidewalk or lost inside a purse—knocked back and forth among a wallet, a paperback, a pencil that stabs the blind hand trying to find her. The lostness is unexpectedly peaceful. Leonora wonders, calmly, if the woman is in love with Jon. Or maybe Jon is in love with the woman. Then the voice returns, apologizing. The phone slipped out of her hand. She's wearing mittens. The voice is too loud and too clear now. Leonora holds the phone away from her face and says something sympathetic. Yes, it's so cold out.

She agrees to come to the precinct where Jon is being held. Her boss is off the phone now. He gnaws on a stick of beef jerky and stares intently at the screen in his palm. Leonora sends him a text and watches him swipe it away impatiently without reading it.

She calls a cab to take her downtown, because this seems like the proper response to an emergency. Instantly, the car is locked in traffic. The money accumulates on the meter in neon red numbers. Leaning her forehead against the car

window—cold, greasy with other foreheads—Leonora tries
to persuade herself that she's a tourist. A visitor, at least. That
the people on the sidewalks are not the same crowds she
observes every day from the office window, when bodies and
bikes and cars are just shapes moving at different speeds.

The desire to speak to Julian appears. Leonora knows
it will eventually subside, but with her face pressed against
the window, pressed toward so many strangers, it seems to
her that there will be a kind of ecstasy—at least, a kind of
honesty—in seizing the desire as it swells.

Leonora has not spoken to Julian in three or four
months. She wrote a polite email of congratulations after the
election. The politeness, so incommensurate with the old
intensity of their emotions, was in its way a kind of rudeness.
He wrote her back right away to say he'd call her—soon—
and he never did.

The phone rings for long enough that Leonora becomes
aware of just how near her desire is to despair. Then he picks
up, and his voice is full of surprise, which is easy to mistake
for happiness. She says *where are you* instead of *how are you*,
because it's a more manageable question.

"I'm at IKEA," he says.

"I'm in traffic," she says.

He is sitting in a simulacrum of a child's bedroom. The
rug, he says, looks overvacuumed. The pillow is dented with
the shape of a stranger's face.

"How many people buy this exact room?" he wonders.
"How many people come in and say, I'll take the whole
thing?"

Leonora pictures him looming over the miniature furniture. He sits down in a small chair and it vanishes underneath him. Leonora clenches her jaw, as if she, too, must bear the unfamiliar weight.

"Who would say that?" she asks.

The cab inches into a large intersection, its front half blocking the crosswalk. A man in an elegant overcoat pounds on the hood and mouths something profane.

"I'll tell you the secret of a good campaign," Julian says, in a voice that is probably supposed to sound conspiratorial. He has always been good at saying things as if he has never said them before.

"Okay."

He is quiet for longer than she expects, and in the background she can hear the sound of small children—the sound of a playground or a swimming pool, a sound that is so generic it is neither ugly nor pure, but always not quite real. When he speaks again, Julian's voice has lost the shiny sound of performance. It's sad.

"The secret isn't getting people to want you. It's telling people they want you and then getting them to forget you told them."

The stream of pedestrians separates when it encounters the cab, as if the car is a heavy rock in a river, and merges again on the other side. The light turns green, but still the car is stuck. Two women walk around the cab in opposite directions. When they reunite, they exaggerate their delight, laughing.

"I'm happy for you," Leonora says. It seems possible this is what she has been calling to say, but once she has said it there is no release. What she had hoped for was the feeling of something coming into view—the feeling when you find the constellation someone has been pointing at, or when you understand the optical illusion someone has been trying to explain. The feeling when it becomes impossible to unsee what before you could only imagine.

"Thanks."

At last the car begins to move. There is not much more for either of them to say. When they hang up, Leonora imagines the effort it will take him to stand up from the chair made for a child. Her phone buzzes with a message from Jon.

They let me go.

Maybe Julian sways a little as he gets up, his balance not quite lost or found, his head momentarily weightless. Or maybe he stays where he is, knees pressed close against his chest. The car inches forward out of the crosswalk.

OLD HOPE

·

When I was about halfway between twenty and thirty, I lived in a large, run-down house that other people thought was romantic. There was a claw-foot tub with squeaky knobs, and philodendrons that draped over the banisters. The door to my bedroom was at least twelve feet tall. I installed a coat-rack over the top, and whenever I needed to retrieve a jacket or a towel, I stood on my desk chair, swiveling uncertainly.

There were six of us in the house. We were all about the same age, and at some point during the summer—I had moved in at the beginning of March, when the mornings were still cold, veins of ice glittering over the front steps—this became claustrophobic, unbearable. The house smelled of sweat and bike tires and something at the back of the oven being charred over and over again. Two boys lived on the top floor and another lived in the basement. (They weren't men, not really.) I was aware of being surrounded. Shirtless, they cooked big vats of tomato sauce, the steam beading on their faces and clinging to the fur in their armpits. They smoked bongs they didn't clean and returned my books warped by bathwater.

One afternoon, while a desk fan whirred near my cheek, I composed a long email to my high school English teacher, because I remembered him as handsome in a remote way. The school had been large and impersonal, full of unkind sounds: the clang of lockers and the terrible screaming bell. But the English teacher wore expensive clothes and took an understated pleasure in saying inspiring things. In my head, he belonged at a prep school. My idea of prep schools came from outdated novels. A *Separate Peace*, that sort of thing. Later, at college, I learned that going to these schools entailed a lot of lacrosse and furtive blow jobs, and that, too, became a kind of romance in my head.

I calculated that the English teacher was about forty, and then I pressed send. The email covered a lot of ground. I summarized what I called my "college experience" and devoted a long paragraph to *The Artist's Way*, the self-help book that I was using to structure my days. I described the cat outside my window, which I took the liberty of calling a feral cat. Toward the end of the email, I found myself saying that I couldn't understand the fear of death. Maybe it was a boy thing. The male ego. If death turned out to be anything other than pure oblivion—if the afterlife was even a little bit lucid—I would be disappointed. Wasn't everyone looking forward to the chance to actually, finally rest?

One evening, at a Chinese restaurant with my friend Max, I debated whether to tell him about the email. All the tables were occupied, so we sat on the sidewalk out front, eating from plastic containers. One of the tables inside was pushed right up against the window, and occasionally I made eye contact with the woman sitting there, only inches away. Her boyfriend leaned his head against the glass, his curly hair flattening like something compressed in a microscope slide.

I put an entire dumpling in my mouth and wondered if Max would think the email was *in character*. I had been asking myself this sort of thing more often. I knew I should permit myself uncharacteristic actions, but when I did act—and in general, I thought about acting more than I acted—I wanted to know if I was acting like me.

"Or the person recognizable as me," I said out loud.

"What?"

"Never mind."

Max bit a small hole in one end of a dumpling and dribbled soy sauce into the opening.

"Hannah says she's at the point where she would consider getting pregnant to be a sign."

Hannah and Max had been dating for a year or so. She was an avid reader, with relatively few opinions about the things she read.

"A sign of what?" I said. "That it's meant to be?"

"Or just that it's time."

I imagined Hannah in maternity clothes. She was small enough that the billowy tunics would make her look even smaller.

"She isn't actively pursuing motherhood, but it's a future she knows she wants," Max said. "So why not now?"

"Motherhood is a pursuit?"

The dumpling slipped between his chopsticks. Ambition alarmed Max. For years, he had been saying he was going to find a new job.

"I only like thinking about the future because it hasn't happened," he said.

I nodded while I finished chewing. "Happening spoils the fun."

It's difficult to say whether I expected the English teacher to respond. For as long as I can remember, I have heard been told *Don't get your hopes up.* My mother said it habitually, about even the smallest form of desire. The faintest glimmer of wishful thinking. She said it when I wondered if the roadside diner offered free refills, or if my father would send me a Christmas present. She said it when I applied to every college I had seen mentioned in books—the ones with demure colors, Latin mottoes, things called quads.

There were graver threats she might have worried about. Student debt and callous boys. Rising sea levels. But it was disappointment, most of all, that she feared for me. For a long time, her fear seemed like a form of doubt, maybe even an insult. Proof that she didn't think I could weather the minor calamities that life had in store. I would have preferred, I thought, that she imagine me as a tragic victim—someone susceptible to plane crashes and sexual harassment. But she didn't worry that I would die or be destroyed. She worried that I would crumple in the face of everyday failures, that I would gradually deflate—a quiet, unremarkable hissing— into a case of unfulfilled potential.

And so while I waited for a response to my email, the worst-case scenario I imagined was a standard reply. *Hope this finds you well.* No reply at all would be better than that.

When the English teacher wrote back, I was distracted. The college I had attended was in the news. A nineteen-year-old boy had died at one of the fraternities. The stories about the tragedy had a unifying effect among those of us who were not directly involved. I began emailing with friends I had lost touch with, whose lives were hard for me to imagine. They had good salaries and reliable boyfriends, with whom they bought reasonably sized pets. They circulated Facebook petitions for uncontroversial causes—cancer walks and hurricane relief. I disdained them, and was aware that my disdain was born of dislike for what these friends proved about me: that whatever I was doing—cultivating a taste for chipped mirrors and monochrome palettes, reading self-help books that scorned other self-help books—was a life of ugly indecision, pooling like day-old rainwater.

In our emails, we asked the same questions too many times: What did we know back then? What should we have known?

The English teacher's reply wasn't any of the things I'd feared it might be. He wrote without preamble. He taught at a new school in a new city. It was a Quaker school, which was apparent in only small ways. There was no dress code and no student government. Lofty words, called tenets, were painted on the walls in big block letters. *Equality. Simplicity. Environmental Stewardship.*

Once a week, the school convened for Meeting. Like

chapel, except everyone sat in silence. The chairs were arranged in concentric circles, with an empty space in the center. There was no preacher, no text, no assigned seating. Most of the students were Jewish. Anyone was allowed to speak, but sometimes the Meeting passed in uninterrupted silence. *If you're moved to share* was what the real Quakers said. The implication, presumably, was that God did the moving. But the students interpreted these instructions loosely. The results were beautiful, often breathtaking.

They spoke about all kinds of things. One told a story about his grandfather, who was dying in a different country, and another wanted to talk about his baseball team—its first time in the playoffs. A third explained that he was making a list of all the ways to categorize people. Crest or Colgate, Apple or Android. People who joke about farts and people who don't. People who say *I love you* at the end of every phone call and people who can barely bring themselves to say it at all.

If there were only adults in the room, the English teacher said, all this vulnerability would be a performance—the art of carefully calibrated disclosure.

Then the email ended, as abruptly as it had begun. He did not include a sign-off, which was the sort of thing I thought about a lot. *Best* or *All best* or *All my best*. He just wrote the first initial of his first name, a name I had never called him.

I resolved to seek advice about the English teacher's email, but as time passed and it remained in my inbox, crowded with other, more straightforward messages, the strangeness of it came to feel like a kind of intimacy. I was afraid of what discussing the intimacy might do to it.

Max texted that he was coming over: he needed help.

Instantly, I relaxed. I would have to make the email small and insignificant to accommodate his problems. This task made me energetic, like a sudden burst of resolve to clean utensils that have sat in the sink, their dirtiness turning into rebuke.

Max perched on my bed and untied his shoes slowly. He arranged the shoes under the bed. His fastidiousness seemed ominous, so I asked him if Hannah was pregnant.

"Of course not. She's on the pill."

I nodded. "She's conscientious."

"She doesn't even set an alarm to remember," he said admiringly. "She just does."

Max was very handsome. To those who doubted that my feelings for Max were uncomplicated and platonic, I often added: *objectively* handsome. But when he spoke in tones of awe, he seemed ugly.

"Well, she said if she *did* get pregnant."

"That conversation stood for a larger conversation." He sounded impatient. "It wasn't, like, practical."

We sat there quietly for a little while. In general, I prided myself on understanding the true meaning of things. I looked at Max's sneakers, their laces coiled neatly out of view.

"What's the real problem, then?" I said, when I had recovered.

The problem was that Max couldn't stop imagining Hannah having sex with strangers. Or not-strangers. Men or women. Anyone, really, who wasn't him. It had gotten to the point, he said, that he had to conduct these fantasies during sex in order to stay turned on.

"Do you close your eyes?" I said.

Max shook his head.

"I don't imagine *she's* someone else." He swung his feet back and forth, the way a child might. "I just imagine *I'm* someone else."

"It sounds exciting," I admitted.

He looked at me gratefully. When he leaned back on the bed, his shirt rose up, revealing the gentle incline of his stomach. I might have touched it, if it weren't so difficult to convey the difference between tenderness and desire.

"Did you ever have imaginary friends?"

"A lot," he said. "An old man named Leo. And an orphan whose name was all vowels."

"I had an orphan, too!"

"And sometimes the ghost of Leo's wife."

I had photos of Max as a little kid. Bowl cuts and big cheeks. The same eyes. It was easy to love the little kid. Max looked at the ceiling, where the remnants of a glow-in-the-dark solar system clustered around the overhead light.

"I yearn for my childhood," I said. "But everyone says I seem old."

"That's because children don't yearn," Max said. "They just want." The adhesive on the stars was slowly coming off. A comet's tail wilted, Saturn's rings peeled at the edges. "They want *stuff.* Popsicles. Yogurt in tubes."

"Is the fantasy with Hannah—"

"*For* Hannah."

I squinted, which I hoped conveyed skepticism. "Is that yearning?"

Max shrugged. He stood up carefully, the mattress sinking and shifting under his feet. Wobbling, he reached up toward the stickers, but the ceiling was still far away. His T-shirt rose even higher when he lifted his arm. The comet tail dangled out of reach. Like everyone, he looked strange from below.

"Yearning is so religious," Max said, bouncing gently on his heels.

"It is not."

When I thought of all the ways faces rearranged themselves from different angles and distances—a nose in profile, a nose up close, a nose illuminated by a camera's flash—it seemed miraculous that we recognized each other at all.

"Fine," he said. "It's so *spiritual.*"

"Don't say it like that."

When Max sat back down, the bedsprings whined.

"If I say I'm looking for a way to make Hannah an object of my desire again—" He stopped swinging his feet.

"Does that mean you're objectifying her?"

"I want to be a good guy."

We sat there silently for a while, not looking at each other, which could have meant that Max wasn't a good person, or that no one was, or that we wanted to sound smart and goodness was the kind of thing that always came out sounding dumb.

Sometimes in the morning there was a star or an orb or a planet's ring on the pillow beside me. I had to remind myself not to make everything into a metaphor.

.   .   .

I wrote the English teacher again on a Monday. I told him that the fraternity had me thinking about things that travel in packs. Big cats and protesters and cans of soda. The visual element interested me. Seeing these things on their own became sad, sometimes even alarming. Lone-wolf shooters. A table for one. A single can of beer in a paper bag.

High school is the ideal time for packs, I wrote. Everyone is weak, everyone wants strength in numbers. Once a critical mass has assembled, the vying begins. Jostling your way to the front.

What counts, I asked him, as being alone? In the mornings, I could hear the whir of someone's electric toothbrush through the wall. On the subway, I misjudged the space between two passengers, pressing myself against the shape and warmth of unfamiliar thighs. And who was that man I saw every week—sometimes every day—on the same platform, waiting for the same train? I noticed when he wore a new red coat, but I didn't know his name.

Every few weeks, I saw Hannah jogging in loops around the park. I went to the park to read or call my mom on the phone, but if I saw Hannah I felt aimless and guilty. I made myself do a dozen push-ups, or the kind of sit-up where you pedal your feet in the air.

One weekend, I stopped and sat under a tree beside the running path, and then I saw Hannah twice. On the first loop, she didn't say anything—just waved and went on running. On the second loop, she slowed down as she approached, jogging in place for a little while. Her face was blotchy with exertion, but she wasn't sweating very much. This made her seem pretty—full of restraint. She had taken her headphones off when she got close, and a pop song leaked out of them.

"Hey," she said.

"Hey."

She didn't turn the music off, and I could hear the song building toward its last ecstatic chorus. They were lyrics I knew without knowing how. She spoke over the tinny, far-away sound. We didn't say anything interesting. How many loops she'd done, what I was reading, whether the cool weather was here to stay. She put the headphones back on before saying, "Are you sleeping with Max?"

Her face had almost returned to its normal color.

"Of course not."

She stood there a few moments longer, bobbing her head to the music, or just to her thoughts, and then she was running again. I sat under the tree, waiting for her third loop, but she didn't reappear. I saw a dog walker, a cycling team, a group of toddlers all holding the same rope. The song got stuck in my head.

The last time I saw the English teacher, we were sitting in his office, in between the chemistry lab and the girls' bathroom. As is true of life, but not movies: I didn't know it was the last time.

That year, my handwriting had transformed abruptly. Until then, I wrote in vigilant cursive: *m*'s with three humps, *g*'s that didn't look anything like *g*'s. These inefficiencies seemed elegant, until suddenly they seemed absurd. In my cautious world, this counted as a revelation. Afterward, I didn't write so much as scrawl. I was known, by then, as an overly conscientious student, and most of the teachers ignored the illegibility of my new handwriting. One of them, leafing through the pages of an assignment, said, "I can assume you're saying something correct in here, right?"

The English teacher, of course, was different. He called me into his office that day and said he couldn't read a single word of my final exam. He held out the small stack of blue books. The class was about tragedies. We were always saying things like, "But is it *tragic*, or just *sad*?"

"Here," he said, flapping the books in the air. "Read them to me."

I read the essays haltingly at first, since the words seemed to accost me: they had never been intended to be said aloud. I paused after a few paragraphs. I would have chosen differently, I said, if I'd known I was going to perform. The English teacher didn't respond, and so eventually I continued. He watched me carefully. Didn't smile a fake smile or nod encouragingly. Already I was imagining how I would describe this—in writing, maybe, or to a friend who didn't actually exist. *Our eyes locked.* I pictured solid, clinking metal.

I began to read with more confidence, changing words here and there when I saw a sentence headed toward a clumsy conclusion. These adjustments made me feel artful—adult. When I finished, I was out of breath, my face prickly with adrenaline. I waited a few seconds before I looked up, allowing myself the thrill of being watched. The words on the page were a faded graphite streak; they were or weren't the same words I had spoken.

When I did look up, he was unbending a paper clip in his lap. I couldn't see his face.

"Ow."

He dropped the paper clip on the ground. His finger, reflexively, went between his lips. He met my gaze then, but he seemed distracted.

"So," he said. "What grade should I give you?"

There was no longer anything pleasurable about his inscrutable expression. His mouth twitched or his eyes flickered, or maybe I just imagined that he was moving farther and farther out of reach.

"I don't know," I said, looking at the floor, the mangled paper clip on the carpet, grey on grey.

"What do you deserve?"

He twirled a pencil around his thumb and his pointer finger. It was a habit the boys in class all copied. Boys who slouched and argued, boys who took their sneakers off under their desks.

"Nothing much."

"Nothing much," he repeated, turning over the phrase, as if it were extremely interesting, or unbelievably stupid. "B plus? B minus?"

I said nothing.

"C plus?"

I was an A student.

"Okay," I said. I held out the books, which weighed almost nothing. "Do you need these back?"

He shrugged. On my way out, I threw them in the trash.

A few weeks later, I graduated, wearing a robe in primary blue. The teachers wore blouses or ties and uncharacteristically nice shoes. I never found the English teacher in the crowd, though I remember waiting for him—and telling myself I wasn't waiting—until nearly everyone had left. I watched the football field gradually emerge from under so many feet. Clumps of kicked-up dirt, the puncture wounds of high heels.

There was a garden behind my house, but it was mostly plants that flourished of their own accord: wisteria and honeysuckle, clover and scorpion grass. For a few weeks each year, a blanket of crocuses. "Technically," I told Max, "they're weeds."

I wanted to plant something new—something intentional—so we bought paper envelopes full of seeds. The man who sold them to us said they'd never grow. Already, the weather was changing. Max nibbled the bottom of a honeysuckle and sucked.

"The problem with horticulture," I said, "is the more you know, the more things you're obliged to dislike."

We pressed the seeds into the soil and covered them up. They were small and easy to misplace. Some blew away in the wind. I planted tomatoes, because I wanted to see something ripen on the vine.

We sat on the ground and Max plucked onion grass absentmindedly.

"Do you know about peppers?" he said.

"What about them?"

He took off his shirt and wiped his hands on his stomach. He was wet and shiny, and the grass from his palms clung to his skin.

"Green peppers and yellow peppers and red peppers."

I took off my shirt, too, and then my bra.

"Yeah, I know," I said. "They're all the same thing."

Max looked at me carefully. There were a few hairs around my nipples, long and dark, like eyelashes in the wrong place. We were sitting cross-legged, and he reached out and held one of my breasts in his hand. I imagined him putting his mouth around it, the image so vivid that it seemed to me I could taste my own sweat. Then Max let go. He wiped his hands again, and I couldn't help thinking that it was me he was wiping off.

The English teacher wrote me one more email, at the very end of the summer. It arrived in the middle of the day, but I was still in bed. I liked the idea of going all day without speaking, clearing my throat sometime in the evening, preparing to address someone for the first time. I had folded a blanket into a person-size rectangle—just enough weight to feel like I was being pinned down. I drifted in and out of sleep and dreamed about boring things. Brushing my teeth, trying to wash the cheese grater and shredding the sponge. When I woke up, I was impatient, and a little embarrassed. I wanted to scold someone: this isn't what dreaming is for!

While I lay there, one of the boys who lived in the attic was moving out. I could guess what he was carrying by the sound of his footsteps. He ran up the stairs three or four at

a time (trash bags, mop), and came down slowly, step by
step (bed frames, picture frames). The new roommate was
arriving soon. I'd never met him, but I'd scrolled through
enough of his social media to decide I didn't object and
wasn't curious.

I looked at the email for a long time without opening
it. The blanket didn't cover my feet, which made me very
aware of my toes. Lying under the blanket, sweating in all
the creases of my body, I told myself that the English teacher
had been cruel all along. In the hallway, plastic hangers clattered. A pillow thrown from two floors up sounded like getting the wind knocked out of you.

Cruel! I repeated the word in my head, trying to approxi-
mate indignation. What does outrage look like, when it
first begins to unfurl? The doorbell rang. The old roommate greeted the new roommate. A few minutes later, they
knocked on my door.

"It's us."

I pushed the blanket away and underneath my clothes
were damp. I pictured Max rolling off Hannah when they
were finished having sex. Both of them on their backs, staring into space. In a second, she would pull up the sheet and
one of them would turn toward the other, murmuring the
usual things, touching with hands that were just hands again.

"Come in," I said, forgetting to clear my throat.

The door opened and I deleted the English teacher's
email. I felt loss and then relief, or relief and then loss. I sat
up. A star did not fall from the ceiling.

SECURITY QUESTIONS

•

On days when she's unproductive, Georgia likes to imagine she's pregnant. That way, she'd be accomplishing something. Dana, the man Georgia is sleeping with, has a wife without a uterus. Years ago, when she still had one, she gave birth to a son. He's the same age as Georgia—twenty-six—and Dana only ever speaks of him with pride.

When Georgia found out about the son, she googled him right away. Tim. The screen on her phone had been broken for months, so she looked at pictures of him through a spiderweb of cracks: a portrait in black and white, a group photo, an action shot from a long-ago soccer game. Dana says they look alike, but this isn't really true. The most you could say is that they both have brownish hair, biggish noses.

For years, Georgia swore that she would never have a day job; all she wanted was to be an actress. She was in movies her friends made and a few plays in theaters the size of living rooms. But now she works at a company where no one is over forty. The company sells fancy meal kits—

individually wrapped ingredients, laminated recipes—that get delivered straight to your door. There's a Ping-Pong table in the office and a petition circulating to replace it with a Foosball table. It's okay to wear shorts, and sandals, too, if you're paid enough: Georgia's boss has stubby toes and hair sprouting like antennae from the tops of his feet.

Tim is a filmmaker. He made a documentary about cowboys and another one about Mennonites—small projects, but well received. In an interview, he says he's interested in dying ways of life. It has been decided that Tim has potential: he's someone who will become a bigger someone. Maybe, Georgia thinks, predicting who will be successful is what men do instead of getting pregnant, what they do when they want to watch and wait—to see what will hatch. Late one night, she streams Tim's first documentary on her laptop. She isn't sure whether she's hoping it will be good or bad, but in the end she's impressed. When she finally falls asleep, her dreams are filled with bearded men and wild, snorting horses.

Debbie never wished she had a daughter until the hysterectomy. One of her coworkers accumulated four sons in the quest for a girl, which Debbie thought was pathetic.

Once, when Tim was young, she said it wistfully, not quite seriously: "One of each would have been nice."

That made Tim upset. Above all, he wanted to please.

"I can be a girl, too," he said, hopping back and forth on one foot.

"No, you can't," Dana said sternly, and Tim stopped

hopping, frozen on one leg like an ungainly bird, his face scrunched up with the effort not to cry.

Debbie had the surgery when Tim was twenty-three. He'd been living in the attic for a while, out of inertia not necessity, but recently he'd found an apartment nearby, in a neighborhood where new parents lived. The lobby of the building was crowded with strollers and miniature plastic scooters—bright pink and blue and yellow, with helmets to match. Tim's apartment had high ceilings and no walls, and he had no idea how to furnish it. Room to grow, he kept saying.

Debbie's neighbor had gone under the knife that same year, and she came over to tell her what to expect.

"Hysterectomies make you extremely constipated," the neighbor said, "and extremely happy."

The pamphlets from the doctors said Debbie might experience a feeling of loss. The doctors themselves said little.

In the neighbor's case, there was no cancer. There were fibroids and continuous, debilitating pain. Her uterus expanded all the way up to her rib cage. Without it, Debbie's neighbor said, her body became a room.

"Like cleaning out the garage."

Later, Debbie repeated this to Dana, who nodded sympathetically, as if it sounded sensible. This wasn't the reaction she was looking for.

"The garage?" she said. "My uterus housed human life. Not a Honda."

"A Ford."

"What?"

"Her husband drives a Ford," Dana said.

Debbie hadn't stayed overnight at the hospital since giving birth. After the surgery, she was tired and sweaty, or else she was tired and parched. Pregnancy had a sound logic: you lost a fetus, but you got a baby. This time, the thing they took out of her was her.

Tim texted: *get well soon.* A few minutes later: *or whenever you're ready!*

A fruit basket arrived at the hospital, even though nothing was in season. Unripe strawberries and melon carved into flowers.

"Imagine a daughter," Debbie told Dana. "I would have been excellent at dealing with girl puberty."

His mouth was full of honeydew. The painkillers made the insides of her elbows and the backs of her knees itch unbearably.

"Breasts feel like tumors at first," she said. "Some girls freak out."

"You mean"—Dana finished chewing—"*you* freaked out." The flower's stem was a sharp wooden skewer.

"They're not soft at the beginning. They're hard lumps."

He poked her thigh absentmindedly with the skewer.

"What I'm saying," Debbie continued, "is I would've given my daughter adequate information." She snatched the stick out of his hand.

"You're high," Dana said.

"I would never have let her mistake growth for death."

.   .   .

Georgia has three sisters. The four of them have curly hair and curveless hips and the same groove between their nose and mouth—a little wider than normal. They all live in different states, but Georgia is the only one in a different time zone. Whenever she thinks to call them, they're already asleep.

She lives alone, in a glass building. Her ex-boyfriend was the one who chose the apartment, because he was the one paying for it. When they broke up, it was because he needed—*wanted,* she corrected him—to see more of the world, so she was the one who stayed. She had a room-mate for a while, to cover the cost. Now she has an empty room and not enough money. To Dana, she calls it the study, or the guest room—whichever sounds better.

The best thing about the building, in Georgia's opinion, is that it has a view of the identical building across the street. There's an apartment that's the mirror image of hers, occupied by a man who wears Bluetooth earphones and expensive-looking slippers. During the day, he works at the counter in his kitchen while various TaskRabbits maneuver around him and his appliances. Georgia has never seen the man having sex—this is always the first thing people want to know—but he seems social. He hosts dinner parties and is often being interrupted by phone calls.

"I'm always the one calling," she complains to her friend. "I'm never the one getting called."

"But we're young," the friend assures her. "Eagerness isn't undignified until you get old."

Georgia and her ex-boyfriend dated for six years. They met during the first week of college and were having sex by

Halloween. Georgia had never had sex before, and she was surprised by how effortful it was—like taking a test. In the moments afterward, her jaw clenched with familiar dread, the certainty that her failure was about to be revealed. Her head was cloudy with anticipation, and when she spoke, her voice sounded thick, not quite like her own. *I love you*, she said, without having planned to say it. Her boyfriend smiled. When he said it back, some dam opened up inside her. Like being drunk, without the nausea.

They began making routines together right away, and soon enough it was impossible to imagine their days apart. They watched the same sitcoms and did their laundry together in the basement of the dorm, sitting on top of the machines while they waited. Once, her boyfriend slid a finger inside her there, the dryer vibrating underneath them. She'd been afraid of someone walking in, but she tried to enjoy it. Later, she found an unfamiliar sock clinging to their clothes. It made a crackling sound when she peeled it away from one of her T-shirts.

When they moved into the glass building, they merged calendars and playlists and underwear drawers. It seemed inevitable that everything, eventually, would follow. Georgia pictured sand on a beach, the grains sifting and resifting with each wave, the same wet grey once the tide went out.

When they first find out about Dana, Georgia's friends ask if he takes Viagra, if his skin is papery. Does she have a code name in his phone? They are disappointed to learn that Debbie knows about the affair. She knows Georgia's last name and phone number. They have never met in person, but Debbie has texted Georgia and Georgia has texted back. With the family-and-friends discount, Debbie has sampled some of the food from Georgia's company: ancient grains, Cornish hens, mushrooms named after instruments. Debbie is also free to have sex outside her marriage, but so far, Dana says, she hasn't exercised the right.

Sometimes, Georgia takes pleasure in the maturity and complexity of this arrangement. The truth is that deception might be more exciting. For a while, Georgia tried to become obsessed with Debbie. She asked Dana questions that might yield covetable information. Does Debbie eat dairy? How many continents has she been to? Is she good in emergencies? What is her biggest regret?

Dana interprets these questions as symptoms of jealousy. He's flattered. He admits that Debbie has discontinued the meal delivery, because there's too much packaging. A duck breast wrapped again and again in Saran Wrap, three strands of saffron swimming in a Ziploc bag. The food is good, Dana assures Georgia, she just can't bear the waste.

Dana's job is something in the boring kind of law. They don't discuss it. Debbie is an architect at a prestigious firm whose work is all over the city. Georgia takes a tour of the rare-books library Debbie helped design, and parks her car outside a house with no right angles. The buildings are not Georgia's idea of beautiful.

"But they're literally monumental," she tells her friend afterward. "I mean, what will *we* leave behind?"

·　·　·

Debbie memorizes sonnets—one, sometimes two, a week—because she's heard it keeps the brain in shape. When she's awake in the middle of the night, she recites herself back to sleep. *My mistress' eyes are nothing like the sun.*

Her memory has always been a point of pride. Debbie never forgets phone numbers or deadlines, never asks for directions twice. Everyone is impressed when she remembers the name of a sibling or a pet.

Dana is the opposite. He forgets Tim's blood type, lets the GPS guide him to the gym. Above his desk, there is a Post-it with all the answers to his online security questions.

What was your first job?

What is your grandmother's maiden name?

Dana claims he was a paperboy, but Debbie suspects this is the warping of nostalgia—romance for a past that was never really his. As the list gets longer, the questions get stranger, as if the project of authenticity has gotten harder and harder to solve over time.

What city would you prefer to live in?

What is the name you almost gave your first child?

The answer to the question is *William*. There is no special story to explain why the name was discarded at the last minute. Will is just an idea, an alternate history that only two people have ever considered. Debbie is calm when contemplating the irreversible course of her life, the forks she can't untake, the things she can't unname. She has never had patience for mothers who wish they could turn back time.

"Parting with something isn't the same as losing it," she once told a woman who cried through every school play.

"Parting!" the woman sobbed. "I want to be whole."

Debbie rolled her eyes.

When her grip on her belongings loosened, she told herself to let go. Tim grew up. Dana traveled, and so did she. Her face—the loose skin over her throat, the downy hair on her cheeks—ambushed her in the mirror. She scolded herself for her vanity. Her beauty had never been hers.

Debbie sits down at her husband's computer, his supposed secrets surveilling her from the wall. It might be nice, she thinks, to discover these passwords and actually need them—to log in and feel the staticky proximity of the unknown. But there is no affair to uncover, no paper trail to follow. Everything is out in the open, where it is vast and cold and hard to stand.

Tim tells everyone he knows about his next film. He hasn't been on a date in more than a year, but he's almost always messaging someone on one of the apps. The women are smart and funny and surprisingly easy to talk to.

"What happened to meeting people at parties?" his dad asks, when Tim explains how the apps work. Dana almost sounds sad. "Or finding people by chance?"

Tim tells the women up front that he isn't ready to meet in person. *Looking for friendship*, one of them says: *I get it.* He agrees, but this isn't exactly right. *You want to fall in love*, another says, *without being in love.* Maybe this is closer to the truth.

The women complain to him about other men on the

app—the photos with cute babies and wild animals, the strenuous attempts at decency and indecency—and withholding his own complaints makes Tim feel virtuous. He doesn't mention his exes or his parents or his neighbors, the newlyweds whom he hardly ever sees but hears all day. They yell and curse, have sex and sob.

Some of the women have seen his documentaries, or pretend they have. Once, a woman in Dublin suggested they watch one of them together, even though they weren't in the same place, even though his evening was her middle of the night. They'd press play at the same time, she explained: they'd text throughout. A bottle of wine and a bag of popcorn for each of them. Tim said sure, but as soon as the opening credits appeared, he turned it off. He considered watching something else—she'd never know—but he couldn't bring himself to lie. She was nice about the whole thing. *I hate looking at pictures of myself,* she said, trying to commiserate. They picked something animated instead—a kids' movie that was supposed to make adults cry. (He did, a little.)

Tim's new film is about a boy who emerged from decades in a coma. It turned out he'd been awake all along. For years, the boy's father took care of him like a saint, changing his clothes, giving him sponge baths, cutting his hair when it grew past his eyes, even though the eyes never opened. Eventually, the father grew old and tired, and he hired a nurse to help with his son. She was the one who said she noticed something flickering inside the boy, who by then was no longer a boy. The miracle awakening followed, with its share of joy and hardship.

It sounds beautiful, one woman says. *It sounds cheesy,* another says. *Thank you,* Tim says to both.

Debbie's sixty-fourth birthday falls on a Friday. Dana calls Georgia to reschedule plans.

"You forgot?" Feeling angry on Debbie's behalf fills Georgia with righteous satisfaction.

"I inverted the numbers," Dana says.

"Friday is the sixteenth." She is sitting cross-legged in the guest room, the walls bare but not clean. "You thought her birthday was the sixty-first?"

"I got mixed up."

The room used to contain an expensive rowing machine, which her ex-boyfriend took with him when he left. Now there's just a futon. When Dana spent the night for the first time, Georgia kept the door to the room closed. Part of her was embarrassed by it—the empty walls, the pillowless bed— and part of her was excited: a secret she was keeping, a future she hadn't unveiled.

"Have you bought a present?"

"Debbie doesn't approve of gifts."

This sounds admirable.

"It's a power play," Dana says. "The moment you give a present, you force someone into debt. The receiving party is always, in some sense, the guilty party."

He explains this coolly, efficiently. For a second, she imagines him in his office, which is nothing like her office. A closet for his suit jacket and his spare jacket, a paperweight on his desk and a prize on the wall. Her own job seems, just then, like a pointless game: the Ping-Pong paddles, the flip-flops, the piles of Saran Wrap clinging to itself.

"What about gratitude?"

"What about it?"

They change their dinner reservation to Saturday, and on Friday Georgia texts her friends. She tries on outfits she hasn't worn since college. She straightens her hair, which she hasn't done since high school. The straightener sizzles each time she closes it, sighs each time she opens it.

"You look like the ninth-grade dance," her friend says when Georgia arrives at the restaurant.

"You remind me of hating myself," says another.

They drink tequila and compare early sexual experiences. Georgia squeezes a wedge of lime until all the cracks in her hands sting.

"Raise your hand if you've masturbated in a library."

"Raise your hand if you've given a blow job in a moving vehicle."

Georgia hasn't, but she says she has. Her friend returns from the bar with two shot glasses in each hand.

"If Dana had a daughter," she says, "do you think he'd still be dating you?"

The morning after her birthday, Debbie listens to all of her voicemails. Some of them are voices she hasn't heard all year. The childhood friend, the college friend, the office friend. The friend from architecture school who pulled all-nighters with her, both of them weeping silently over their cardboard. The friend from a long-ago pregnancy class, whose twins were sucked out of her.

Debbie's sisters—two of them, plus a sister-in-law—leave messages from the car, the yard, the kitchen. A microwave beeps insistently in the background. A baby gets on the phone. *Birfday.* Her sisters are all grandmothers now. They say it's the best job they've ever had, which isn't saying much: they haven't worked since they got married. One of them lives around the corner from her daughter, who is raising three kids—triplets—all by herself, who spent all her savings on fertility treatments that promised just one. Sometimes, the daughter said, you get more than you bargained for.

Debbie's own mother had never pretended to enjoy being a grandmother. She told Tim to call her by her first name. *Let's just be friends,* Debbie heard her tell him once, when he was still a baby. She visited on holidays, wrote him postcards, promised to take him to Istanbul, her favorite place in the world—but she drew the line at babysitting. She'd done her share of parenting. Debbie's father, she said, had been a kind of child, too.

This year is the year Debbie outgrows her mother— turns the age she never reached. Until now, it had been a small reassurance to know that the two of them had undergone the same effects of time. Her mother's life didn't look much like Debbie's: she'd married, divorced, married again; she'd applied for her first job when she was forty years old. But she knew all the things Debbie wanted to learn. How to get from one year to the next, how to wait and weather, how—sometimes—to change. Her hair lost its color. She wore shoes that were good for her knees and clothes that were plainer and plainer over time. She believed in being ready—she had a condo without stairs, a detailed will—and she believed in being honest.

"Aging," her mother said, "means realizing everyone can live without you." A pause, and then she added, "*Will* live without you."

She insisted that she was lucky to get sick before she was really dispensable. Debbie's sisters told her she was still young, and she said—*old enough*. She did chemo and something experimental and then she said stop.

Would her mother have gotten rid of her uterus? Would she have wanted Debbie to get rid of hers? They were different questions, weren't they? Debbie stares at the phone and wishes she could conjure up her mother's voice. Wishing makes her a child again, stranded in a dark room, in a big crowd, on an airplane for the first time. She still has so many things to ask. *What happens next?*

On the night she gets locked out, Georgia hasn't seen Dana for two weeks, and she is glad for the excuse to call. She gave him a key, even though he rings the doorbell every time. It's the beginning of spring, when half the trees are still cold and skeletal and half are bursting pink—cherry trees covered in down, magnolias dropping satin tongues all over the sidewalk. One year, Georgia was caught off guard by the changing of the seasons: she looked up and everything was heavy green. Ever since, she has vowed not to miss it.

She walks up and down the block and calls Dana from under a dogwood tree. She kicks up a heap of petals, browning at the edges like the hem of something dragged through the mud, and she calls again. She sits there for almost an hour before she decides to call Debbie.

They have spoken only once before, and Georgia has thought about her voice too often to actually remember it. It's an efficient voice—a voice good at giving instructions, at making itself understood—but not an unfriendly one. Debbie is hundreds of miles away, at the kind of conference she dreads.

"The hotel shows off for the architects," she says when she picks up the phone. "The shower has six different settings, but I just want *normal.*" She doesn't sound impatient, just tired.

"Where's Dana?"

Debbie takes one short breath. Georgia can hear the hard spray of water in the background.

"He's out with his girlfriend," she says.

There is no particular sympathy in the way she says this, which is its own sort of kindness. Georgia reaches into her pocket one last time, as if the keys will be there after all, as if the whole scene can be undone. Seconds go by while she can't think of anything to say. A second, she thinks abstractly, is a surprisingly long time.

She doesn't call the locksmith right away. She goes to the bar on the corner, even though it's about to close. She's never been inside before, because there is always a sports game playing through the window. It takes Georgia a minute or two to realize that the man at the other end of the bar, half on the stool, half off the stool, is the man who lives across the street in the other glass building. This close, she can see that his face is puffy and his neck is badly shaven. When he goes to the bathroom, he doesn't come back. Georgia takes sips of yellow beer while the bartender wipes a rag in lazy arcs.

"Should we check on him?"

The bartender lifts up the man's glass and Windexes underneath. He shrugs.

The door is unlocked and the man is asleep on the toilet. His pants are still on, his earphones still in. He smiles vaguely when Georgia wakes him up, and lets her guide him to the closest booth. She checks the contacts in his phone. There is a long list of outgoing calls to someone named Ashley and a lot of texts about invoicing. Georgia looks for *Mom* and *Dad*, and then is embarrassed for looking: the man is forty, maybe older.

"Well," she says. "I know where he lives."

The bartender gives her a weird look but keeps emptying the cash register, sorting the wrinkled bills into piles that won't lie flat.

When she opens the man's front door, Georgia knows where the light switches are in the dark. In the moment before she turns them on, it is easy to believe that the apartment will be her apartment—that her water glass will be where she left it, that the closet will be filled with four seasons of her coats. Is it like a dream, or a movie, or a trick of history, to see what appears instead? The man's bedroom is painted dark purple and the blinds are pulled shut. The kitchen cabinets are filled with things in the wrong places: coffee mugs next to frying pans, silverware in the drawer closest to the ground.

The man collapses on the couch. For a few minutes, Georgia sits beside him, staring across the street. It's a pretty apartment—everyone says so—but it's even prettier from here. There is a crack of light beneath her bedroom door, as if someone is home. Her book is tented on the couch—she hasn't read it in days—and the fridge door is crowded with shapes: pictures, postcards, invitations to weddings she won't attend. Eventually, she takes the man's shoes off, puts the keys on the table, and turns off the lights.

Tim goes back to his parents' house every couple of weeks. They invite him for dinner, but he prefers to arrive when there is no particular occasion, when he can catch them in the middle of things. The sink running, the lawn mower sputtering. The glazed eyes of pretending to read the newspaper, the mouthed syllables while clamping the phone between cheek and shoulder: *just one min.* Tim knows he should resist the tempting lie: that watching people when they think no one is watching is the same as seeing the truth.

He goes upstairs while his dad finishes the front page and his mom finishes the phone call. He lies on his twin bed with his legs hanging off the edge, his feet on the ground, because it feels good to be reminded how much he's grown. On the wall above the bed, there's a list of all the movies he watched when he was thirteen years old—one every Saturday night, including Christmas Eve. He takes a picture of the list and sends it to a woman who's trying to make it on Broadway. She doesn't reply, so he sends it to a woman who's a photojournalist in Kenya. He reads the list again and this time it seems pretentious, not cute. He wishes he could unsend the texts. He turns his phone off and looks at the black screen. Downstairs, Tim's parents' voices sound like anyone's voices. He pretends he can tell their footsteps apart, but he can't really.

Tim hasn't finished shooting the new film yet, but he already knows which scene will be the last. The father and son sit side by side at the kitchen table. The father is worrying something in his hands—a paper napkin, maybe, or an old receipt. He looks down at his lap and his son looks straight into the camera. What do eyes look like, after so many lidded years?

The father says he will never forgive himself. There is a moment or two of quiet, and then Tim hears his own voice from offscreen:

"Forgive yourself for what?"

When Georgia sees Dana again, she has been completely alone for two days straight. Half the office has lice; everyone has been sent home. She is used to eating lunch for free, from huge trays of sandwiches with Post-it notes (pickle, no pickle). Her fridge is empty, but she keeps opening it anyway, as if something might have appeared inside.

Georgia expects Dana to say, *I heard you spoke to Debbie.* Or maybe she expects him to say, *Sorry.* He doesn't say anything. When she opens the door, he's staring down at his phone, but when he looks up, he's smiling, his eyes bright and wrinkled at the edges. It's a smile of forgiveness, and though she isn't sure who needs to be absolved—what did she do wrong?—she feels the warmth of it, the childish joy of a fake egg being cracked on her head. They order takeout and watch

a movie he's already seen. They have sex with the curtains
drawn, the room turned into a cave. In the moments after
she tells him he can come, her body relaxes, retracts, waits.
She closes her eyes and imagines herself on the other side of
the wall, in the empty room, the fluorescent streetlamp bathing her in its unforgiving light, the coolness of the half of the
mattress where no one else sleeps. He lets himself collapse
onto her, his breath warm and damp in her ear.

In the morning, he sees the bugs in her hair. He takes
a picture with his phone to show her, but Georgia doesn't
want to see.

"Why not?"

"It's a phobia." She shivers, by way of explanation.
"Insects freak me out."

Years ago, she tells him, there was an incident with pill
bugs. She tells him before she remembers that this isn't true.
Georgia's sister is the one who's really afraid, who found an
infestation when they were kids, who closes her eyes and
swears she can feel them crawling all over her skin. Georgia
doesn't feel bad about the lie. She misses her sisters with a
sudden, unusual intensity, or maybe she just misses the time
when it seemed as if their lives belonged to each other—
when they forgot whose fears were whose, whose stories were
whose, because they were everyone's.

"Rolly pollies?" Dana says in a strange voice. It takes her
a second to realize what it is—the voice you might use with
a child. She can see that he wants to make her laugh, and it
feels good, and a little dangerous, to refuse, like the heady
excitement of holding her breath for too long.

They google on his phone until they find the special

shampoo and the special comb that all the message boards recommend, and then he's gone. She is standing at the window in a shower cap, hands held resolutely behind her back—don't touch!—when he leaves the building. She sees him hesitate for a moment before he knows which direction to turn, the world reordering itself in daylight. She does not expect him to ever come back.

At home, Dana sits on a low stool in the bathroom while Debbie runs a fine-toothed comb through his hair. The stool used to say *Timothy*, spelled out in rainbow blocks, but they've long since lost the letters.

"Are the lice a sign?" Dana asks. "A plague on both our houses?"

"You're only saying that because it grosses you out."

Dana doesn't respond. He reaches up to touch his head, and Debbie bats his hand away. She has made it a rule not to imagine what Georgia looks like, and she is good at following rules. But it's difficult, now, not to wonder about Georgia's hair.

"It turns you off," she says.

"I'm not a switch."

Dana's hair is thinner than it used to be. In a few places, Debbie can see right through it.

"You've always been a switch."

Tim arrives while Debbie is covering Dana's head in olive oil and tea-tree oil.

"We're in the middle of something," she says.

"You could call next time," Dana says.

Some oil trickles down his forehead and lands in the corner of his eye. He blinks a few times. Tim leaves them like that, tells himself to remember them like that—shiny hands, shiny heads, looking for something invisible. He waits in the kitchen, leaning against the unmagnetic fridge. The Broadway actress sends him a picture of her as a baby, grinning in the bathtub, shampooed hair molded into a single spike.

Later, while he's setting the table for dinner, Tim is the one who remembers about the old Hasidic lady—a celebrity of sorts, famous for her method of delousing. When he was nine or ten years old, he says, she cured him.

"That's impossible," Debbie says. "You never had lice."

"We would remember," Dana agrees.

It isn't a holiday, but he's roasting a turkey and mashing potatoes. There's real cranberry sauce—not the kind in the can. It seems festive. Years ago, Debbie insisted he learn to cook, and now he's the only one who does. The recipe is old and stained with the traces of previous attempts, which is somehow comforting: they've been here before.

"It was fourth grade," Tim says.

Debbie refuses to believe it. She lists every sickness he has ever had, every vaccine, every ER visit.

"I remember them all." Her voice gets high-pitched when she's defensive.

"It was your re-honeymoon," Tim says patiently, and his patience makes her ashamed.

"Our what?"

"That's what you called it."

At the last minute, they'd bought a ticket to Mexico. She remembers now—of course.

"The ruins were important for Mom," Dana says. "Professionally."

"We were getting our marriage back on track," Debbie says.

Dana bastes the turkey. It's pink instead of brown—the skin isn't crackling the way he wants it to.

"So, who found the lice?"

"The babysitter. She made me swear not to tell you."

The babysitter was twenty, maybe twenty-five, and Debbie could tell from the start that Tim worshipped her. She cooked hot dogs and buttered pasta. She knew thirteen different card games, plus a few magic tricks. She wore tight T-shirts that showed her nipples, and sometimes her belly button, too.

"Siobhan," Debbie says wearily.

One night before Mexico, Debbie and Dana had gone to an eight-hour movie that they had wanted to see for years. Siobhan said she didn't mind staying late. When they came home, she was on the couch, the TV was on mute, and Tim was curled up in her lap. He was too big for anyone's lap. His limbs were crowded together at ungainly angles, his head bent awkwardly so that his cheek could rest against her chest. He was screaming, Siobhan explained—screaming in his sleep.

Dana squirts the juice all over the turkey and opens the oven again. A gust of heat makes him close his eyes. He stands up and clasps his hands together to avoid touching his hair, which ends up looking a lot like prayer.

"Resist the temptation," Debbie keeps saying.

There are a few uncomfortable moments of silence, in

which Debbie and Tim stare at Dana's interlaced fingers. Like any body part, they become ridiculous when scrutinized in isolation. Swollen and meaty. Then Tim looks up and says:

"Was Dad fucking Siobhan?"

Dana texts Georgia the address of Larger Than Lice, but she goes alone. Their texts are only logistical now.

From what Dana described Tim describing—*my son*, he writes, as if he had never told her his name—she was expecting someone's basement: her head tilted back in the kitchen sink, the smell of someone else's cooking in the next room. But the place has changed—now it's halfway between a doctor's office and a salon. The receptionist wears scrubs and the magazines in the waiting room are up-to-date.

Georgia nearly walks out. She is fragile, these days, when met with her own false expectations. Then a woman in a wig and an ankle-length skirt emerges. She wears a Disney-printed nurse's uniform over her sweater. She could be twenty-five or forty-five, which makes her seem like a sister and a mother all at once.

The woman doesn't explain what she's going to do. She doesn't warn that it will hurt like a pinch when she presses hard into Georgia's scalp, or that it will hurt like a sting when she plucks something out of it. The sensations are all surprises.

"I'm not a masochist," Georgia says out loud.

The woman doesn't respond. Her glossy wig hangs like a curtain over Georgia's forehead.

"I guess I might be."

The comb sends tingles down pathways Georgia didn't know existed. A tendon on the inside of her thigh is connected to the lobe of her ear. This makes her feel well designed—put together.

"The bugs remind you that your body is food," Georgia says in the silence. "That's the worst part, I think. They're not just living on you, they're living *off* you."

Georgia lets herself imagine what's underneath the woman's wig. Hair only one man sees. The truth is Georgia can't imagine anyone coveting her like that—asking her to hide something, longing for the moment when it will be revealed. But it might be nice to have it—whatever *it* is—all to herself. When she's finished, the woman braids Georgia's hair, the way she wore it as a child.

And now that it's all over, where have the bugs gone? Georgia pictures the bodies. Clear exoskeletons with clusters of dark organs visible inside, punctured by tweezers, corroded by chemical shampoo. They might ooze her own blood, the way mosquitoes do. They belong to her, because she kept them alive.

At home, Georgia unfurls the braid. Her hair is kinked all over. She brushes it again and again, until it is alive with electricity, until it radiates out in all directions, quivering with static, the ridges throwing light in all directions, for no one else to see.

MAKE BELIEVE

•

One week after I told Arthur to stop contacting me, I got a job with a celebrity. The job was on a commercial, doing all the things that fell through the cracks. I'd keep the mini-fridges stocked with seltzer and energy bars, find the right-size envelope and the right-color earrings, silence a smoke detector and unknot a stubborn mass of wires. The commercial was for deodorant, or cologne—something to do with pleasant odors.

My own sense of smell is underdeveloped. A man once speculated that this might explain my lack of enthusiasm for sexual conquests. Like dogs, he said, a lot of people go wild in pursuit of a certain scent.

"Like dogs?" I said, and he nodded.

At that point, I had been thinking about the celebrity for several months. I'd had these kinds of obsessions—can we call them companions?—for as long as I could remember. They were generally famous or dead, and sometimes both. They were always men, which I admit was unoriginal.

I had considered what the celebrity liked to eat and how his apartment, large but not opulent, would be laid out. When I left the house, it was always with the possibility of bumping into him, or at least spotting him in an adjacent checkout line. This was implausible, but not impossible: he did live in my city. (Many people do.)

The celebrity was an actor, and it was often said that he had remarkable range. He starred in biopics about assassinated politicians and TV shows about ordinary people living in cramped houses. There was trauma in his youth, which he only ever mentioned obliquely. Something happened, I think, to his brother.

The night before the job started, I was in a crowded bar for the engagement party of a friend whom I no longer knew that well. I found myself talking to a very thin woman, a stranger whose wrists I admired. I imagined her storming off and someone grabbing her wrist. *Don't go!*

We swirled our drinks around and eventually I told her that I was going home early, because of the job with the celebrity.

"You don't have a job with him," she said.

"I do!" I said this with delight, because it was the first time I'd mentioned the job out loud. Arthur was the only person I would have told.

"You don't."

I knew it was an ordinary job, but it felt good to be delighted.

"He died," the woman said, "just this afternoon." She pulled out her phone and showed me the home page of a semi-serious news outlet. The celebrity's name was there, along with some version of the word *death*.

The job had been scheduled to start very early. I had set several alarms, three or four minutes apart, as I did when going to the airport at unnatural hours. And in fact the day before the job was not unlike the day before an important trip. I found it difficult to concentrate and tried to think of ways to fortify my body. I installed an app that reminded me to drink water at regular intervals.

The very thin woman seemed to be sympathetic to my shock, which only made me feel more misunderstood. There had been a public outpouring of grief. I wanted to say, *Do you think I'm just a sad fan?* But to myself I had to admit, *Aren't I just a sad fan?*

In the morning, my alarms went off, one after the other, while it was still completely dark. The streetlamp outside my window had been broken for weeks. The dark felt like a rural dark.

In one of the celebrity's most famous movies, his character is summoned home by a death in the family—the loss of a cruel and complicated patriarch. The character boards a plane in funeral attire. It is hot and sandy where he's going, and he will be overdressed. The plane touches down and you can see the collar digging into his neck. His polished shoes click on a polished floor. The gasp of the automatic doors is also the sound of heat hitting him in the face.

My alarm rang again. I kept my eyes open, because I didn't want to fall back asleep. It's different to picture things with your eyes open. I imagined handing over my belongings at the airport, watching them disappear on a conveyor belt, somehow certain I would see them again, thousands of miles away. In my head, I boarded the plane and breathed the recycled air. In the room, my eyes adjusted to the dark.

I would have liked to feel the lurch in my stomach when the wheels lifted off the ground and the wings took over, but there is only so far a body will go in the service of imagination.

Six months before the celebrity died, Arthur left the city we lived in together, where most of our friends lived, too. Seven months before the celebrity died, I dropped out of school. This was a long and agonizing decision, but not a very interesting one. Many people had made the same decision before me and would make it again after me. For years, I had supposedly been writing about the archive of a famous writer. In fact, I had been doing nothing but reading his letters over and over again, in a room where everyone wore white gloves and spoke in whispers. I knew the names he called his wife and his lover; I knew about the trip to Tangier, about the writer's block, about all the wrestling with God; I knew the difference—slight—between his *r*'s and his *v*'s. Arthur said that in the end I knew very little about myself. My adviser, a man with a white beard and a vague accent, agreed.

Arthur moved to a dense foreign city that was friendly to expats, but not too friendly. Living there would be difficult enough to count as an adventure. He followed a job. I didn't follow him, because he didn't ask me to and he didn't ask me not to, and his indifference frightened me. I was only in the habit of chasing things in my head.

Arthur's job involved selling other people's art, which didn't mean liking other people's art. When we had lived in the same city, I went to galleries with him, where everyone pretended to walk around aimlessly. In fact, everyone had a mission. Arthur was often impatient with the artists for not completing theirs. The collectors, he explained, were looking for a performance. They wore tucked-in shirts and sweaters in presidential colors. They wanted artists who wore fishnet shirts, ripped denim, shoes that looked like robots. They wanted to buy more than just art; they wanted to buy personality.

When Arthur moved, it was unclear if we were still dating, though he texted me a lot. Mostly photos, mostly of dogs. The large public parks in his new city were overrun with them. He had never heard so much barking. Sweating through his office clothes, he became fascinated with the anatomy of canine tongues.

Panting, he texted me. *Incredible technology.*

I read the text and decided to respond in twenty minutes. He texted again.

Why do we keep our tongues in our mouths?

I took a shower to pass the time. Eighteen minutes later, I said: *So we can talk!*

What was most striking about the parks, Arthur said, was that they were frequented by purebreds and strays in equal numbers. Some of them had elegant noses and humanlike hair that touched the ground. Others had more skin than fur, taut pink patches where they scratched until they bled. He sent me a picture of a greyhound getting his teeth brushed. Later, a pit bull with sagging nipples and a shredded-up ear, like paper ripped out of a notebook. There were ornate fountains in the park. Cherubs spitting, pissing, glinting in the sun.

The photos were probably supposed to mean something. It was tempting to think they meant *missing you*, but it would have breached the terms of our intimacy to ask. We knew better than to take pride in wordless comprehension, but we did it anyway.

When the celebrity died, I went back to looking for odd jobs. I learned this approach to employment from my friend, an aspiring artist. He told me that everyone he knew—other aspiring artists—worked this way. *Cobbling things together*, he said. I told him I wasn't sure if I was entitled to be a cobbler. I had never made any art. He smiled pityingly and referred me to my first job, walking a pair of miniature Australian shepherds. Before the walk, I fed them each a Prozac, crushed into a dish of their favorite meaty stew.

Most often, I found work as a personal assistant. I learned this could mean many different things. A woman with a laryngectomy wanted me to sort her extensive jewelry collection. Her neck hole wheezed while she watched me untangle delicate silver chains. She made me empty my pockets before I left. Later, a young couple with a tiny apartment hired me to do their grocery shopping. Sheepishly, they asked if I would wait on them during dinner.

"It's like"—the husband looked at his wife instead of looking at me—"make-believe."

"Growing up, Travis always wanted a butler," she said.

They unfolded a card table for dinner, which blocked the route to the bathroom, but they tipped generously. For dessert, I unwrapped Klondike bars and served them on plates.

The jobs were usually short-lived, and most weeks I found myself in new parts of town. Arthur once explained to me that some cities expand up and some expand out. Vertical sprawl and horizontal sprawl. If you can, he said, pick a vertical city. They encourage optimism.

Our city, which was now just my city, had skyscrapers and many-story walk-ups. There were pharmacies and grocery stores in old bank buildings, where the vaulted ceilings were fifty feet above the shelves. I had been in elevators with uniformed operators and elevators with no buttons at all. Somehow they already knew where you were going.

Three months had passed when I answered an ad for a night nanny; the celebrity had long since stopped appearing in the news. My sleeping schedule was already out of whack. I liked scrolling through my feeds in the dark, when I could be sure that only strangers were awake. Nearly everyone I knew—the number seemed to be dwindling—lived in the same time zone. Increasingly, they believed in regular bedtimes. They adjusted their screens to glow soothing orange at night and wore expensive mouth guards that made them lisp.

While my known world slept, I read old tabloid articles about the celebrity. The smallest developments of his life were resurrected on my phone: he starred in a new movie, he found a new girlfriend, he bought a coffee. *Just like us.* Sometimes the headlines said that the celebrity was exhausted. In the world of famous people, I learned, this was a clinical term.

When the celebrity was alive, I had avoided this kind of behavior. I wanted to know him, not to know things about him. This had felt like a principled distinction. Now that he was impossible to know, I investigated him, collected him. At strange hours, when late-at-night became early-in-the-morning, my greed managed to look like something else. My phone a bright square in a dark room, pretending to be a portal or a treasure or at the very least a time machine.

To become a night nanny, I took the train uptown, to a luxury apartment building with a view of all the best museums and the reservoir in the middle of the park. The doorman had to swipe a special card to take me to the twenty-sixth story, where the elevator opened directly into the front hall. There were no shoes or coats in sight. There was an end table with a fan of reputable magazines and a framed handwritten letter, presumably from someone famous, though I didn't recognize the name.

I was interviewed by the mother and three other women. The day nannies. They asked me questions while we observed the plate of cookies between us.

"Did you have a formative caregiver?" the mother said.

She seemed disappointed when I told them what little I could remember of the years I had spent in daycare.

The girl was five years old and her name was Susan, which seemed to me like a name for adults. The first nanny explained that Susan didn't respond to Sue or Susie. Terms of endearment were off-limits.

The mother left in the middle of the conversation, reappeared in flattering gym wear, then left again. The father was mentioned only once. He alone, the third nanny explained, was allowed to say *sweetie*.

It was Susan herself who showed me the twin beds where we would sleep. She told me I could keep my pajamas under my pillow.

"Or bring them in a tote bag," she said solemnly.

Each day, I relieved the day nannies around the time Susan brushed her teeth. She wore nightgowns, or a onesie with the feet scissored off. Otherwise, she said, wearing it made it hard to breathe.

"I want to wiggle my toes," she said, and I told her I understood.

While Susan slept, I searched the Internet on my phone. Every several hours, I calculated the time difference between Arthur's city and mine. The silence of these nights reminded me of the silence of libraries. It wasn't as peaceful as it sounded; I had long since stopped trusting this kind of quiet. In my second year of working in the archives, there had been a major announcement: a celebrated painter's love letters were about to be unveiled. The letters were mostly to her husband, an even more celebrated photographer, and she had insisted that they be sealed until fifty years after her death. I respected both the painter and the photographer, and I thought this suspense seemed romantic, proof that some love really did endure. But on the day of the unveiling, I had forgotten all about it. I arrived at my usual time with my usual supplies—sanitizer and snacks, a thermos wrapped in plastic, to prevent spills—and there was a line around the block. I watched from across the street while the line inched forward. People chatted, laughed, craned their necks to see the front of the line. Their giddiness might have been inspiring—it isn't every day that a library attracts a crowd—but instead it seemed to me like an indictment. I took notes and met deadlines, but when was the last time I had been so excited?

At Susan's, I hardly slept. In the morning, when it was time to leave, a car was waiting for me. It was sleek and black, with miniature water bottles in the backseat. The first time it picked me up, I finished all four bottles in quick, desperate gulps, and the next day there were eight, wedged into the cup holders. Mortified, I never touched them again.

Often, I went weeks without seeing Susan's parents. I heard the elevator open late at night. They made the sounds of rich people. Heels on hardwood, keys to luxury vehicles on custom-cut marble. Where did they learn to murmur like that?

Once or twice, the noise woke Susan up. She peered at me from across the room. In the dark, she seemed even less like a child.

"It's them," she said.

I nodded. My phone lit up on my chest. I pictured my chin glowing bluish, and just then it was intolerably sad that Susan had never seen me in the sun.

"Her green boots," Susan said.

"What?"

"I can tell from the sound."

We listened to the feet click.

"No you can't," I said.

Susan looked at me silently for a few seconds, and I could

tell I had betrayed her. She turned away, her face to the wall. On my phone, I had found the celebrity's sister's Instagram, where she posted pictures of her children—twins. In one, taken when the twins were still infants, the celebrity lifted the babies in the air as if they were barbells, grinning sheepishly at his biceps. I scrolled back one year, then another. Before the sister had become a mother, her account had mostly featured photos of unpaired gloves, found on the street. Abandoned, muddy, flattened by tires. The hashtag #seekingsoulmate had attracted an enthusiastic following.

In the kitchen, the fridge opened and closed. Susan didn't toss or turn or snore. Was she awake? I wondered if it was my job to keep her asleep. I could hear things that didn't belong to me rattling, clinking. When they spoke— people I could barely picture, voices I couldn't quite make out—I longed to be closer to them. My face felt bare and prickly, like someone had recently touched it, like someone had whispered so close the words were whorls on my skin.

A few months after Arthur moved away, he called and woke me up. It was late morning, nearly noon. I had missed my first alarm and then my second, along with a text from my roommate asking if we had any baby powder. There were ants in the kitchen. None of this really mattered, since I had nowhere to be, but my head swarmed with regret.

Arthur was calling to tell me he was dating someone new. The straightforwardness of this embarrassed us both. We disliked discussing predictable events. The truth, of course, was that I was desperate for the small details of his life, and now of hers. When I pulled open the shades, there were hundreds of bugs marching down the side of the window. In the fierce light that streamed in, it was easy to imagine someone who possessed everything I lacked. In my head, she was a doctor or a teacher—something passionate, but important, too. A lavish cook who never dieted, the kind of person who wasn't afraid to arrive at a party alone. She posted earnest things online, without wondering who would see them. Naked and tangled in a bed I'd never see, she knew how to answer when Arthur said, *Tell me what you want.*

"Does she speak English?" I asked him.

They spoke in her language, which I had hardly ever heard him use. A few years earlier, on our way back from a long trip, we had stopped for a day and a night in their city, back when it was not yet their city. I was surprised by how loudly Arthur spoke in Spanish, like he was selling something—shoving words into other people's hands. I listened to him barter for a bag of spiced nuts. I was a little bit disgusted.

Later, sitting on a bench near the hotel while Arthur went jogging, I was turned on by the thought of his voice in a different language. An ugly dog investigated my foot and I ignored him. I pictured my face pressed into the mattress and Arthur's hand pressed into my back. When it was over, he would murmur words I couldn't understand. There would be parts of him inside me I couldn't see. This was what I liked best about sex—possessing something we couldn't even be sure existed. I hated the sight of semen. Smeared on my thighs, dribbled on my stomach. Milkiness inside a condom, like a bag of something forgotten at the back of the fridge.

The dog nudged my sneaker again. His breath on my ankle mocked my fantasy. I frightened myself by wanting to kick him. His leaking nostrils and undisciplined tongue, his swollen testicles, knocking back and forth.

After dinner, Arthur hailed a cab, something foreigners were discouraged from doing. He insisted the danger was overblown. I didn't necessarily agree, but I assumed this was how other people's adventures came to be. The car was small and white, and there was a palm-size hole in the floor. I watched the asphalt speeding by until I felt sick. It was surprisingly mesmerizing.

Arthur couldn't understand the driver. He's speaking too fast, he said. Too much slang. He pressed his forehead against the glove compartment in distress. I covered up the hole with my shoe, to stop myself from watching.

The cab dropped us off at a hotel I didn't recognize as our own, and it became clear we didn't have enough money for the fare. Arthur presented his credit card. The driver looked at the plastic, unimpressed. Arthur checked his pockets a second and third time. He said we were only a few dollars short, but he didn't meet my eyes. Eventually, he got out of the car, assuring the driver he would be right back. I wondered if he noticed he was speaking English. He went into a nearby convenience store, and when he returned, he was holding two loaves of bread and a liter of soda. He passed the items through the passenger-side window. By then, he had collected himself. *Lo siento.*

Back in the hotel room, Arthur kissed me and held my face gently between his hands. He said flattering things that I couldn't make myself believe. His fingers smelled bad, like coins. I was surprised I could smell him at all. I tried my best to think about sex, but instead I thought about the loaves of bread. I pictured the slices palmed into perfect balls, swallowed with Coke straight from the bottle. I pictured sandwiches with multiple meats and sandwiches with nothing but mayonnaise. I pictured them abandoned under the front seat, green then grey then black.

I turned away from Arthur. I apologized in a language I didn't understand, mimicking his accent, and it made me feel a little better—a little less like myself.

The day after the celebrity's funeral, an ex-girlfriend of his had announced that she was pregnant. She was, as far as her fans knew, currently single. She did not elaborate; she let everyone speculate. Some people were made ecstatic by this news. The ex-girlfriend, like the celebrity, was extremely attractive, and this seemed to be cause for celebration: the mixing of two auspicious gene pools. Other people were outraged. She was smearing not only his name but his legacy.

I didn't believe the ex-girlfriend, but I thought I understood her. I, too, could feel the celebrity rattling around inside me. The kick of a heel against my ribs would have been a comfort, because it would have made it real.

Ever since I had quit school, my period had been behaving irregularly. It came three weeks in a row, or else it didn't come at all. When Arthur left, I told the gynecologist—he had the same vague accent as my adviser—that I wasn't having sex, and he nodded with stern approval. He told me to

eat fortified cereal and sleep eight hours a night. I was supposed to keep track of my period with an app, which also
let you keep track of your mood—a smiley face or a frowny
face—and your pain. You could choose between one and
four lightning bolts. I ignored the app and kept track of the
ex-girlfriend's pregnancy instead. In pictures, she wore tight-
fitting maternity clothes and cradled her stomach. I could
see her belly button through her shirt.

I had been a nanny for only a month when the ex-
girlfriend was spotted in Cancún—her stomach huge and
in the sun—with a man no one recognized. He had good
hair and impressive abs, but he wasn't famous. Apparently,
he was the father. I read a few headlines that I couldn't bear
to click, and never learned his name. A few days later, my
period came, more brown than red. I wrapped a tampon,
swollen and smelling, in layer after layer of toilet paper and
buried it in the bottom of Susan's trash can. Lying in bed,
I drifted in and out of sleep and dreamed that she found
it anyway. She was cupping something red and dripping in
her hands, something that looked a little bit alive. In the
morning, I fished the tampon out and brought it home in my
purse, because I didn't want her to be afraid.

One night—what became the last night—I arrived and
Susan was not in her pajamas. She was wearing a floor-
length dress, which she held an inch above the floor, revealing a pair of white patent-leather shoes. The day nannies
were clearly upset. The three of them had already packed
their bags. One of them summoned the elevator impatiently.

"It doesn't come faster if you press it more," Susan said, sounding a little haughty, though mostly sounding sad.

"You're not the mother," the nanny said.

"I'm not the mother," Susan repeated, which was not a retort at all, and left us with nothing to say.

She dropped the hem of the dress, and it was only then that I realized it wasn't something made for a child. It was a woman's cocktail dress, sleeveless. The armholes stretched down to Susan's waist, so I could see her ribs and the elastic top of her underwear. She didn't have a round stomach, as it seemed to me all children should.

When the elevator arrived, Susan ran inside, the dress dragging on the floor. The door began to close and fear flashed across her face. She held out her arm, which was hardly more than a twig, to stop it. She reminded me of the trees that get delivered to desolate city blocks—trunks that are more like branches, entire root systems bagged in burlap, half a lifetime before they'll cast any shade.

The elevator door didn't stop when it encountered Susan's arm, so she put her whole body in its way. She did this without any desperation. Twenty-five floors below her, unthinking metal on either side.

The day nannies dropped their bags and jumped into action. One of them blocked the door and another grabbed Susan with both arms, pulling her back into the apartment. She looked awkward in this embrace. Her body wasn't built for absorbing into anyone else's. It collapsed neatly, like a chair that advertises how little space it will take up in the closet. The elevator closed, unaware of whether it was empty or full, buzzing faintly while it descended.

It seemed suddenly perverse that so many hours would pass before I was on the ground again, that so many of my nights took place at a dangerous height. The windows were required by law to be unopenable. What kinds of lives elevated themselves like this?

"Let me go," Susan addressed her nanny's elbow. "I'm already late."

The nannies unbuckled Susan's shoes instead of responding. Susan pedaled her feet in the air, kicking their wrists halfheartedly.

"Where are you going?" I asked.

She glared at me.

"Don't monitor my whereabouts."

"Okay," I said. "Do you know when you'll be back?"

Susan licked her thumb and rubbed the patent leather ferociously. She began to cry.

"I don't know," she said. The shoes clattered onto the floor. She gulped for air while she cried. Her mouth seemed unjustly small.

"Breathe," the first nanny said.

"Breeeeeeathe," the second nanny said.

They took long, exemplary inhales.

"Do the thing," the third nanny said.

Susan looked at her for a few seconds. Then she cradled her arms around an imaginary bundle and began to rock it back and forth. She released a long, rattling breath, and stared resolutely at the nothing in her arms.

"Self-soothing," the first nanny whispered to me.

"Take care of the baby," the second nanny said, patting her heart illustratively. She had impressive, maternal-seeming breasts. I wondered if my flat chest was an advertisement for my professional incompetence. Could everyone tell I lacked a spiritual compass? I wore flimsy things called bralettes. I had never disciplined my imagination.

"There's Gatorade in the fridge." The elevator dinged to announce its return, and the third nanny held it open for the other two. Her forearm was exceptionally strong. Her veins looked like the stems of wildflowers. I imagined them coursing with blood and, implausibly, milk. "Rehydrate after crying," she said. Then the doors shut and they were gone.

Susan was looking at me when I turned around. She shivered from exertion, but she wasn't crying anymore.

"It isn't real," Susan said, holding out the baby.

I nodded, but I lifted it out of her arms anyway.

"I have to leave soon," she said.

I looked tenderly at the inside of my elbow.

"But you'll be back," I said, swaying gently back and forth.

"Maybe."

"Will you miss us while you're gone?"

Susan circled her hands around my wrists. They were warm, just as they should have been. She wrenched my arms apart before I could stop her. I flinched, and felt stupid for flinching. We stood there for a moment, looking at the floor, or at the baby on the floor.

"Don't be silly," she said, and we went to brush our teeth.

WANTS AND NEEDS

•

The summer Val turned twenty-five, her sort-of stepbrother, Zeke, came to live with her in New York. He was nineteen, and when he appeared at her front door, two pairs of shoes dangling from his backpack, drinking greedily from a can of Coke, she was meeting him for the first time. Decades ago, Zeke's mother had been married to Val's father.

In the evenings, Val came home from work—wet armpits, Band-Aids falling off blisters—and Zeke told her about his childhood. He was raised with mantras and stir-fries and a hot tub in the backyard. His dad submerged himself in the tub twice a day, the jets turning the water the same opaque white as his chest hair. For ecological reasons, Zeke's mom took sponge baths while listening to an app that played thirteen different kinds of rain. Spring rain and winter rain, rain on concrete, rain on sand, rain on tarp, rain on jungle canopy. In their part of California, droughts were common, and sometimes it was illegal to use the garden hose.

For every story he told, Val did the math to match it up

with one of her own. He sailed across the Gulf of Mexico the same year she didn't get a prom date. His parents showed him how to help with the ropes, hand over hand over hand over hand. He broke his left wrist while she was in college and his right wrist during the first lonesome spring she lived in Queens, when every crocus—they'd come too soon—was another false hope.

In exchange for memories, Val dispensed worldly advice. She told Zeke that water pressure was one way of assessing wealth. If he'd gone to college, she said, he would have learned about shower shoes. She bought him a pair of stiff rubber flip-flops from the bodega on the corner and told him boys should use conditioner, too.

One morning, Val heard Zeke having sex with her room-mate through the thin bathroom wall. She turned off the water just to be sure. She stood for a while under the inter-mittent drip of the showerhead, watching the lather slide off her stomach, listening to their heavy breathing. Later, Val explained to Zeke that the roommate was from a famously wealthy town in Connecticut. The master bathroom in her parents' house had a urinal and a bidet.

"This whole thing," Val said, gesturing to the spack-led walls, the unmounted mirror, the houseplants in their cracked soil, "is just an experiment for her."

"So are you," she added.

Val took Zeke to a dinner party with eight types of cheese and one enormous salad. The guests were all women.

"Tell them your mom does Tarot," she told him. "They'll love that."

They passed around wine and made jokes about being salad girls.

"Don't let yourself become a parody," one of them said to Zeke, her hand on his arm.

"There are so many parodies," another agreed, as if they were talking about an infectious disease.

Zeke ate three plates of salad while the women discussed a mutual friend. The friend had recently started working as a high-end escort.

"She gets paid to wear a plunging neckline and eat expensive sushi."

"Not sushi," said another. "Steak."

"There's no physical contact involved."

"The men just want a dinner date."

"Men never *just* want anything."

Val watched someone carve away the rind on a wedge of Spanish cheese. "The wax is edible. You can eat it."

"I don't want to eat it."

"The men are the pathetic ones," someone else said, spearing a tomato emphatically. "Doesn't that make her the powerful one?"

Later, when Val and Zeke were sitting on her couch— scratchy plaid, a relic from someone's grandfather's office— she made fun of them.

"Every single person at that dinner party is a glorified receptionist," she said.

"Aren't they your friends?" Zeke asked.

She hesitated. "I guess so."

For several years, Val's job was reading and rejecting movie scripts at a prominent production company. The scripts came from teenagers and convicted felons and grad students brimming with ambition. At first, Val wrote them long and involved rejection letters. By the end, she didn't write them at all. She met the salad girls at some point during this slow, perhaps imperceptible, slide. They were worldly. They'd been to Oxford and to the opera, they knew the right adjectives for wine. Every once in a while, they proposed starting a book club. Most of all, they complained about their jobs, and they knew how to make complaints into stories. The boss who ate his earwax, the boss who melted butter in his coffee, the boss who ordered his kids a dog from Florida, then returned it within a week. (One of the girls wrote the email requesting a full refund, citing frequent urination and a high-pitched bark.) If the stories were especially funny or especially sad, Val wrote them down in a small black notebook.

By the time Zeke came to live with her, Val had become a paralegal, and she, too, had learned the art of the story. For a while, it had been a small, reliable pleasure: to unfurl each detail in just the right sequence, to hold the girls' attention and be rewarded with their conspiratorial laughter. Eventually, the conspiracy grew boring—she stopped writing things down—but she kept complaining, anyway.

The couch was small, only slightly larger than a love seat, and she and Zeke sat with their backs against the armrests, their shins nearly touching.

"The sad thing is, I wish I were bold enough to answer

Craigslist ads," Val said. "You know, to do something ill-advised."

"Something memorable," Zeke said.

"I take pride in not clicking on Internet ads," she said.

"What's wrong with that?"

He rolled them a joint, which Val said didn't count as illicit, because his dad had taught him how.

"All my rebellions are fake."

Zeke wore a hemp bracelet and a hemp anklet. Val had snipped off his hemp choker with a pair of nail clippers shortly after he arrived. She said only teenagers wore chokers.

When Zeke wasn't wearing a shirt, Val couldn't help staring. *Pectus excavatum,* he said—a concave chest. It looked like something had been scooped out of him, or else like something had been pressed into him. His chest sunk inward and his ribs popped outward, like an overturned rowboat. Val was surprised by the urge to touch it. She looked down at her own chest, dismayed by the weight of her breasts.

"My parents couldn't handle another fuckup," Val said.

Zeke mumbled agreement while he sealed the joint with his tongue.

"Do your parents even believe in fuckups?"

The smell of weed brought Val's roommate out of the kitchen. Zeke swung his feet onto her lap. His boxers were old, the elastic curling away from his waist like a sneering lip, and from a certain angle Val could see his scrotum, more grey than pink. Eventually he disappeared into the roommate's bedroom, and Val stayed on her half of the couch. The roommate giggled on the other side of the door.

While she listened to them laugh, Val traced a scar above her kneecap. On bad TV shows, the victims of crimes were always identified by moles or scars in strange places, places only someone who really knew you would have seen. Val had looked for distinctive markings—a freckle in her armpit, maybe, or a birthmark inside her thigh—but she never found anything. Everyone could see the scar on her knee, and even she couldn't remember what it was from.

When Val was eighteen, her older brother had tried and failed to hang himself. Her high school graduation was only a few weeks away. Her teachers exempted her from final exams, and one of her friends said it would have made a great college essay.

Val's parents consulted a family therapist, and a half-hearted reckoning followed, in which Val and her brother learned about their father's previous marriage for the first time. The therapist said that secrecy was toxic. Reluctantly, her father told them the story of meeting his ex-wife, Naomi. They were at a campground in Colorado, he said, both of them ankle deep in a stream. He was washing his sandals and she was panning for gold. In all her life, Val had never seen her father wear sandals.

Val's brother contacted Naomi right away, hoping to find someone who would share his resentment toward his parents. In the end, Naomi was a disappointment. Her emails were sporadic and badly punctuated, sentences and half-sentences strung together with ellipses. She said she turned on the computer only once in a while, and it frightened her every time: an animal whirring to life. Naomi said that she had sat with her anger and no longer harbored any ill will toward her ex-husband. Maybe his presence, she wrote, was more difficult to endure than his absence. She mentioned her husband and son, but never by name. The emails got shorter and the ellipses got longer and eventually the messages stopped coming.

Val made no effort to get in touch, and several years went by. Occasionally, she told people about her long-lost, not-quite stepfamily for the sake of a good story. *Tell us one thing we wouldn't guess by looking at you.*

Years later, Zeke was the one to reach out. He sent Val a message on Facebook, which she checked more often than she liked to admit, monitoring the whereabouts of her ex-boyfriend's ex-girlfriend. Val told herself this was an inventive form of surveillance—born of something less like jealousy and more like curiosity. At least she wasn't wasting time on *him.*

By then, Val's brother had moved to San Francisco and Bali and North Dakota. He had worked at a frozen-yogurt shop, an ashram, an oil rig. Student debt notices and jury summonses piled up at addresses he no longer remembered. Inevitably, he returned to their parents' house, where his bedroom—the guest room—had been painted dusk rose, or dust rose, no one could ever remember which. He stored his clothes in a suitcase and left cash for the electricity bill in the kitchen whenever he could, even though no one asked him to. His mother said, *Make yourself at home,* but he insisted: *I'm just a guest.*

To Val, a stepbrother sounded refreshing. In Zeke's old

profile pictures, he peeked out of a tent and grew a scraggly, adolescent beard. He leapt into the air, fingers grazing a Frisbee. He pinned a white corsage on a girl's satiny waist.

Val decided she was tired of cultivating her own complexities. Maybe they didn't actually exist. She let a few days go by, and then she messaged Zeke back.

One afternoon in the middle of August, when the fancy parts of the city had emptied out, Val and Zeke rode the Staten Island Ferry until it got dark. It was her birthday, but she didn't mention it. Tickets were free and the view was good. She brought a bottle of wine, which turned lukewarm after one round-trip journey in the sun. Val had imagined there would be something luxurious about this tedium. The other passengers would get off and get on, beholden to some invisible, meaningless imperative—to go somewhere, to get somewhere. There would be something impressive, she thought, in their determination to stay put, to oversee the herd of arrivals and departures, to stretch out across the seats when the deck emptied out, to pass the wine back and forth.

The truth was that the men smelled of beer and the children of sunscreen. The engine idled noisily. Trash rustled underneath the benches. The wine got warm and conversation slowed. Every time someone held a phone aloft to take a picture, Val imagined it falling overboard, swallowed up in the curdled white wake.

They ate eggplant Parmesan and two fist-size meatballs at the only restaurant within walking distance of the ferry station, and when they got home Zeke began to vomit. Val stood outside the bathroom door uncertainly, listening to the sound of him gagging. The faucet ran for an entire minute. When Zeke emerged, Val thought he looked yellow and somehow shrunken, but maybe she was imagining it.

He puked three more times that night. In between the second and third times, Val bought him a liter of fluorescent Gatorade and a package of curly straws. The fourth time, she opened the door even though he told her not to. He was mostly coughing up mucus, flecked here and there with black eggplant skin. His back was cold and damp to the touch. When he turned to look at her, his eyes were desperate—fear that made him look either extremely young or extremely old. She took the fear to be honesty, and was filled with bitterness for all the other faces that had refused to reveal themselves to her. She rubbed Vaseline into the cracks of his chapped lips. She overdid it. The skin around his mouth glistened.

It was a twenty-four-hour bug, and Val felt guilty for wishing it would last longer. Her roommate came and went, changing from one outfit into another into another. Office clothes and gym clothes and a dress that showed her whole spine. Zeke didn't appear to resent her indifference, so Val resented it on his behalf.

She had called in sick to work, expecting a gradual recuperation, but by the afternoon Zeke had regained his strength.

"I'm good at bouncing back," he said, shrugging.

He took off somewhere on his bike, and Val had no

excuse when a friend invited her for coffee. Waiting for their drinks, they observed, as they always did, how many store-fronts had opened in recent months. Her friend had ordered something frothy with unnamed health benefits. The first several sips of Val's coffee tasted chemical.

"Have you told your parents that Zeke's living with you?"

Val crinkled a packet of raw brown sugar but didn't open it.

"I've been googling pets on Craigslist at work," she said, without looking up. "Do you think that's a fireable offense?"

"Val."

"What? They aren't even related to him."

Beside her, a middle-aged woman crumbled her scone to a fine dust and talked loudly into her cell phone. "My only advice is don't ever work at a prison," she said. "You're a prime candidate for falling in love with an inmate." The woman flattened several crumbs with the tip of her index finger.

"*I'm* not even related to him," Val said.

The rest of Val's coffee went cold fast. Her friend's drink was nearly gone, but in between sips she blew on it anyway.

"You're in no position to own a dog."

"To rescue a dog."

"I'm not judging you," the woman said into her phone.

"What does Zeke want from you?"

"It isn't like that."

"Okay," her friend said. Her empty mug was stained bright yellow.

"Cut it out with this savior stuff," the woman said. She pounded the table, but no one turned to look.

.   .   .

After her brother's suicide attempt, the family therapist gave them all homework. The first assignment, he explained, was to practice expressing their wants and needs. He showed them a stack of cards, half of them labeled *I WANT*, half of them labeled *I NEED*. He'd filled a few of them in with examples:

New clothes

Democracy

"Some of them are personal and some of them are global," the therapist said. "Soon you'll be able to make your own."

They took the cards home and Val spread them out on the kitchen counter. Her mother mouthed the words silently:

A *dog*

A *psychiatrist*

Val's father picked a card up.

"Praise and affirmation?" He laughed a mean laugh.

The next week, he lashed out at the therapist. They weren't paying this much for toys.

"Not toys," the therapist said. "Tools."

Sometimes the therapist asked Val what she was feeling, but she never said much. Mostly, she drew patterns in a sand tray with a miniature wood rake. When her mother squeezed her hand, she squeezed back. Val didn't know the last session was the last session, but there wasn't time to wonder why. She went off to college, which everyone said made them very proud.

. . .

At the end of August, Zeke spent the weekend with Val's roommate in Connecticut. Val texted him too often. He said everything was *fun* or *wild* or *dope*. He said the bathrooms were elegant but small. He hadn't seen the urinal or the bidet. After that, Val doubted herself. Maybe it had all just been a rumor. She sat in front of her portable fan until her cheeks tingled, wondering how many of her memories could be corroborated by reliable witnesses. How many were hers alone?

On Sunday, her texts turned from blue to green. Where were they, wandering in and out of cell phone service? Val pictured romantic scenes from movies. When she ran out of ideas, she googled *professing love in film*. She checked the weather in Connecticut to see if it was raining. In the best love scenes, it was always raining.

Val wondered if this was jealousy, but she didn't really want to be a part of Zeke's romance. She didn't have the energy to be involved in the story she imagined for him. The story that took him from one coast to the other and maybe back again, that involved detours and dead ends and split-second decisions, that did not involve plans, because he believed what he had been told: it was the journey, not the destination. She resented him for believing in clichés, and envied him, too. Experience confirmed that kissing in the rain looked better than it felt. Water filled your mouth, dripped off your nose like snot.

The fan broke while the sun was setting, the sky watermelon pink. When Val masturbated, toggling between You-

Tube clips of cinematic kisses and bookmarked porn, her sweat soaked into the couch beneath her. The cushions turned from light beige to dark beige. She imagined Zeke sweaty, too—liquid pooling in the basin of his chest. She imagined her roommate bent over him, sipping from the basin. It was hard to find a place for herself in the fantasy. She imagined licking the sweat from their faces or their armpits or the creases behind their knees, but this just made her laugh. The only thing she could picture was sitting—cool and dry—in the corner of the room. She finished distractedly and closed the laptop, which by now was almost too hot to touch. What kind of person, she thought, fakes an orgasm to herself?

Val went to the bar without showering. The bar three blocks away instead of the bar on the corner, to convince herself she was making an effort. There were votive candles on all the tables and garnishes in all the drinks. Thinly shaved radishes, purple and green. The bartender looked relieved when Val ordered the cheapest can of beer. She bought him a shot of whiskey and he made her a cocktail that smelled like charcoal. She bought him a shot of nicer whiskey.

The couples in the bar leaned over their candles, as if they were warmed by the tiny flames. Confiding in each other, nursing their drinks impossibly slowly. The woman next to Val let the ice in her cocktail melt into fingernail squares. The next time she took a shot, Val threw her head back ostentatiously. The alcohol found its way into her nostrils and burned.

When the bar was finally closed—the surfaces wiped down, the sticky pour spouts left to soak in glasses of blue soap—Val had sex with the bartender in the refrigerated walk-in where the kegs were stored. Underneath his shirt, the bartender had a bird of prey tattooed across his chest and, below it, the lines of a poem she had seen all over Instagram. He sucked her neck and she worried about it leaving a mark. The cold made her less drunk. She tried to muster energy or abandon, and the effort made her even more sober.

While they were getting dressed, Zeke's text arrived. A picture of the urinal—clean white porcelain, a golden drain. *You were right.* Outside, the bartender checked the lock twice and pulled the grate down behind them. When he asked for her number, Val thought about saying no, and then she said yes, already wondering how much time she would spend responding to his texts, then avoiding them altogether.

You're always right.

And why was there no pleasure in that?

That whole summer, Zeke never once asked about her parents. Val didn't mention her brother, and it occurred to her that there were hardly any clues he existed. A Polaroid of them as kids marking her place in a novel she hadn't read in months. A contact in her phone. What a mean reward, she thought, for his survival: to be scrubbed out of her life anyway.

She wanted to explain them all—she wanted Zeke to understand them all—but she didn't know where to start. Her father ordered cereal when they went out to breakfast. Her mother hated opening gifts in front of an audience. Her brother had a photographic memory, which he insisted was a curse. So much clutter in his head.

Who were these people, collaged together from her own partial memories, from scraps of details with glue stick smeared purple on the back? They sounded like characters from the salad girls' stories, nameless figures moved around on a stage. She pictured all four of them in the therapist's office, from above: the moles on her dad's head, her mom's silver roots, her own ponytail pulled too tight. Did her brother have long or short hair? A shaved head? For the first time, she felt not angry or sad but sorry.

"My mom's saving up for a rhinoplasty," Val told Zeke one night while they were drinking seltzer and getting stoned.

"A what?"

She didn't answer. Their seltzer crackled. She wanted to make him feel this—how much she would miss her mother's face, how much she wished for her to be happy—but already she knew that whatever she said would be incomplete.

"Never mind." She finished the seltzer too quickly. Her throat stung. She burped loudly, so he would laugh.

When Labor Day arrived, Val offered to throw Zeke a going-away party, assuming she would have to provide the guests. But Zeke had friends Val had never heard of. A boy with unlaced skateboarding shoes. The owner of the bagel shop down the street. A woman her mother's age. Val felt betrayed.

"I can't serve a teenager booze," she said indignantly, pointing at the boy in sneakers.

"*I'm* a teenager," Zeke said, perplexed.

She stayed in the kitchen for most of the party, pouring stingy drinks for whoever wandered in from the living room. A liter of Diet Coke erupted in her face. The hot apartment got hotter and hotter. Zeke opened all the windows, then gave everyone permission to take off their shirts.

"Not that you need permission."

The bagel shop owner's pectoral muscles reminded Val of supermarket chicken. One woman had an appendix scar, another had a belly-button ring. Eventually, everyone went off to a bar, and then Val was alone. She took a cold shower in the empty apartment, so she could imagine her pores contracting. She hated knowing that her skin was full of holes.

Val was taking big, effortful breaths—the cold made her lungs feel stiff—when the door opened and Zeke came in. The shower curtain was mostly transparent, with a map of the world in bright colors. She hid her pubic hair behind South America. His shirt was half on, one arm hanging out of its sleeve.

"Are we going to kiss before I leave?" Zeke said.

Val turned the water off.

"You're drunk."

"I'm not."

"You're my brother."

"I'm not."

Already, the heat was probably making her skin expand. She pictured the oil underneath it—yellow and industrial, like something you'd submerge french fries in. Zeke came right up to the shower curtain, pressing his nose into Greenland. His eyes crossed, staring down at the trembly line of its coast, and then he looked up, straight at her.

"You've thought about it," he said. "Admit it."

The grout between the bathroom tiles was grey with the beginnings of mold and there were orange rings where bottles had once been. A list of tasks took shape in Val's head— steel wool and liquids that burned where they sprayed. The list reassured her.

"What does thinking have to do with it?" she said angrily, staring determinedly at northern Canada.

Zeke stepped back, and for a moment Val felt herself rush into the space that had opened up between them. Her nakedness thrilled her. Her breasts looked good, the way they usually didn't.

"I can tell when you're thinking about it," he said.

And just like that her longing collapsed. She hated him. Hated that he was young and skinny and unironic, hated above all that he had made it so easy to say: *You don't know me.* She could see the back of his head in the mirror behind him, the whirl of hair at the base of his neck. She could see the parts of him he couldn't.

The morning after they didn't sleep together, Zeke didn't miss his plane and didn't text her when he landed. Val never asked him to keep in touch. She cleaned the bathroom.

Things went back to normal.

She moved on.

Neither version was true, but Val tried to choose between them anyway. To figure out which one sounded better— backward or forward.

Sometimes, on the way to the subway, she experienced

a moment of panic, convinced that her own movement was only an illusion of the bodies in motion around her. She walked the rest of the way with her eyes on her feet, proof that each step was getting her somewhere. At the station, she bought a new fare card every day, even though it was more expensive that way. It helped, to ask and receive.

It was summer again when her brother emailed her. She had a new ceiling fan and a new roommate. In the email, he told her he'd bought a ticket to California, where he knew someone with citrus trees and a fuel-efficient car. There were fires all along the coast that year. Val read about them jumping over highways and looked at pictures of hills turned volcanic orange. The day before her brother's departure, his friend's house had burned to the ground. He went anyway. He read the news from an air-conditioned motel room. There were homemade signs on the side of the road and at the grocery store, thanking the firefighters. *First responders,* he wrote—*isn't that a good term?*

Val didn't write back for a few days. It rained for a long time in New York, which seemed unfair. She closed all the windows and let the air inside the apartment get hot and stale. There was a website that showed the movement of the fires in real time, and Val watched the screen for hours, orange and red dots blinking, growing, engulfing everything they touched. In a dream, she rang the doorbell to her own house and everything crumbled to ash. When she woke up, she took off her clothes, damp with sweat, and checked the fires. The page loaded slowly. *Please,* she thought, and hated herself for thinking it, *don't let them be gone.* The rain collided with her window. The dots danced in the dark.

BRENDA

•

Brenda lives in a trailer, in the driveway of the house she bought and razed and gave up on. The trailer has recently been cleaned and there's tea lisping on the miniature stove, because one of her students is coming by. While she waits, Brenda scrolls through the afternoon's major headlines and checks the expiration dates on the items in her minifridge. There's milk and fake milk, a nub of butter, yogurt with a pool of yogurt water in the center.

    The college where Brenda works is small, unbeautiful. Cinder-block buildings and a cafeteria that serves outdated things—Jell-O cups and croutons in every salad. She walks to class. What Brenda teaches is called creative writing. Not so long ago, it was called creative nonfiction, but the *non* frightened people off. The department head, a woman with silver hair and one elegant pair of earrings that she wears on all occasions, likes to remind Brenda that genre bending is fashionable. She says *fashionable* with a certain weariness.

Men, she says with the same weariness, wouldn't take a class called *memoir*.

On the first day of this year—her sixth year of teaching—Brenda announced that office hours would take place at her house. This is an unavoidably personal class, she told her students, by way of explanation, which is true. It is also true that Brenda avoids her office more and more: her colleagues and her deadlines, her dirty keyboard and her notebooks warped with spilled things.

In general, Brenda's students fall into three categories. There are students with very dramatic lives, which they write about honestly, and poorly. They have endured floods and wars, big plots, evil characters. One of them has a long-lost sister. Then there are students who believe they have dramatic lives, who write at length about small mishaps and deliver the meaning of their stories—the meaning of their lives—in two or three concluding sentences. It is through these stories that Brenda comes to know the names of family pets and the predictable twists and turns of divorce proceedings. Finally, there are students whose greatest fear is that they have no drama at all. They come to Brenda's office and tell her they have nothing to say—nothing worth saying. They write long, precise paragraphs about objects—a papaya, a riverbed, an old man's chin—to avoid writing about other things. What they avoid most of all is plot.

Brenda likes these students best. She puts check marks in their margins. *The slippery meat inside a melon.* She insists: everyone has a story to tell.

.   .   .

When Brenda and her boyfriend Sam moved here, they worried about everything they were leaving behind. They had only ever lived together in big cities where there were thousands of restaurants, where the airport—the water—was never more than half an hour away. Sam could do his job from almost anywhere and Brenda, it seemed, from almost nowhere. There were only so many teaching positions. They took what they could get. The college was near the desert and near the mountains, but the town itself wasn't much to look at. Gravelly yards and dinky pools, kids on fat-tired bikes careening through red lights. For the first few years, they rented apartments, buying new plants every time they moved. They couldn't believe how affordable it was. Brenda filled an extra closet with blue jugs of water, because everyone had warned her about the tap. Like drinking pesticides, her students told her. The second worst in the country, they said, with a hint of pride. The plants, Brenda thought, all looked a little like weapons: sharp spines, leaves that could have been shields.

The realtor saw them hesitate. The future, he said, was a place they could choose to go. They smiled in spite of themselves.

They signed the papers, demolished the house, and stood transfixed by the size of the hole in the ground. There were a few good months. When the rain turned the hole muddy, they stomped in puddles like kids. They hammered with nails clamped between their lips and stepped on each other's steel-toed boots for the pleasure of not feeling.

They couldn't get enough of construction metaphors: knocking down walls, building a foundation. The sound of power tools revving to life was joy and fear.

"Like getting high," Sam said, when the power saw had gone quiet.

"No," Brenda said, sawdust in her hair and her eyebrows. "Like being alive."

Then, last year, Sam left. He bought a plane ticket to New York, where his sister and her husband lived in an apartment they couldn't quite afford. They were ambitious and always tired. They didn't have an extra room, but they had a couch.

There was no especially good reason for leaving. Sam cried more than Brenda did. He might have been crying from guilt, or from pain, or just from the surprise of saying secret, unkind things out loud—the surprise of being a person you can't admire and can't escape.

It was impossible to keep building after that. The tarps flapped noisily at night and there were nails everywhere. Brenda made the trailer clean and spare, stared out the window while the light faded and the wood and bricks turned into ominous shapes. Suddenly, the metaphors were ugly. All they had really been doing was digging a hole.

The student coming to see Brenda doesn't have any parents. When Casey was a child, they were murdered by accident, emerging from a fancy cocktail bar, mistaken for someone else. She was raised by rich, unfriendly grandparents. There is more death, presumably, on the horizon.

Brenda pours dark red tea and Casey assesses the trailer. "It's cozy."

"You're polite."

Casey's mug features three cartoon dogs with pink tongues. In matching pink bubble letters it says *Who Rescued Who?* The mug was a present from Brenda's mother, who is devoted to a small terrier she found on the side of the road. Casey has brought her latest assignment in a pocket folder, printed on sturdy paper. Her essay includes the facts of her life, written in the third person, efficiently and unsentimentally. *Casey was born in 1998.*

When she first started teaching, Brenda did everything she could to cure her students of their fear of failure. There are no wrong answers, she told them. Things aren't *good* or *bad.* The students teased her, in a nice way. Some of them mimicked her soothing, maternal voice.

"Okay," Brenda says, pressing the warm mug against her cheek, "what about the first person?"

Casey looks uncertainly at the pages in front of her. *Casey was orphaned in 1999.*

"Will that make it better?"

"Probably."

She used to say clichéd things and she used to believe the clichés. She used to tell the students the world was more forgiving than they thought.

With a dark pen, Casey crosses out her name in every sentence. She is diligent, eager to improve—an ideal student, by most measures. When she's finished, the page covered with *I*'s—Brenda thinks of I-beams, an invisible metal skeleton—they review the notes that Brenda has written in the margins. She wishes she could tell Casey that these notes are small and unimportant, but this would undermine her authority. If Casey were a little less conscientious, Brenda might respect her a little more.

Later, when Casey is gone, when the sky is still grey and rainless and the tea bags have shriveled up, like dead leaves or the empty brown shells that cicadas leave behind, Brenda drops them back into her mug. They swell into their old shape, fat and heavy and red again, even though the water has long since gone cold.

For the first months that she lived alone, Brenda heard nothing from Sam. She added his last name in her contacts, to remind herself of all the other Sams she knew. One night, she found a website called howmanyofme.com.

"There are 54,591 people with Sam's exact name in the country," she told her mother on the phone. "First and last."

"Hm," her mother said. Brenda could hear the dog barking, the sound of its nails on the kitchen tile.

"Don't say what you're going to say."

"What am I going to say?"

"Oh, you know." Brenda held her breath for a second. "Like, we're all unique."

"Well," her mother said, while the barking got closer, "we are."

Then, half a year after he disappeared, Sam called for the first time, his whole name appearing on Brenda's phone. It was February, and it wasn't raining as much as it should have been. She was intentionally burning two slices of toast. On a hot plate, she let an omelet crisp around the edges.

Disappeared wasn't the right word—out loud, she said simply that he had left, a boring and unevocative word. But how else could she explain why every morning she woke up with a start, in the middle of a plotless, frantic dream in which she looked for him everywhere—in the closet, in the recycling bin, in the trunk with old towels and jumper cables—and never found him?

The phone kept ringing and the burnt toast jumped in the air. She didn't pick up the call, but she watched the lit-up screen until his name vanished. Brenda had always liked things overcooked: the bitterness of blackened bread, the toughness of meat more grey than pink. Sam always insisted raw foods were sophisticated. Nice restaurants served bloody steak, silky fish, dishes whipped and emulsified so all you had to do was swallow. The most elegant desserts were always soft. Brenda buried her phone underneath a pillow and scraped the omelet onto a plate.

After that, Sam called once a week. On different days, but always in the morning, when she was brushing her teeth or steeping her tea, when she hadn't yet said a single word out loud. In the end, this was the thing she couldn't bear, that he would be the first person she spoke to. She started paying attention to how quiet her days were, filled with unostentatious sounds—the faucet running, her feet shuffling. A black walnut fell on the thin aluminum roof and she jumped.

Brenda imagined him calling from noisy places: subways, playgrounds, Starbucks. She imagined him calling from a crowd. The kind of place where you couldn't hear yourself think, the kind of place where you might get lost. Brenda never picked up and Sam never left voicemails. Instead, he wrote to her after he called, emails that all began the same way. *Sorry I missed you.*

Brenda's favorite student is Emily. In October, she submits an essay about fetuses. Recently, she was prescribed a powerful drug for acne. Her doctor, a man with bushy eyebrows and a large Adam's apple that bobs while he speaks, told her not to get pregnant while taking it. Emily uses condoms and doesn't have that much sex anyway, but even so, the idea of the fetus obsesses her. The problem with the medication is that it suppresses certain hormones, which would mess up male development in utero. The dermatologist wasn't clear about what, exactly, would go awry.

"Maybe it would be effeminate," he said.

"Feminine?"

"Sure."

"And what about a female fetus?"

"What about it?"

"What would she be like?"

"Normal, I guess."

"Girly?"

"I'm a dermatologist," he said impatiently.

Emily wanted the prescription, so she stopped asking questions. On the walls of the doctor's office, there were huge photos of pimpled chins and baggy eyes, faces splotched like gourds.

When she pictures the fetus, she pictures perfect skin. Thin and milk-colored, like a hard-boiled egg, with black-olive eyes, aquatic feet, and a blank space where the penis would be. The blankness is his best feature. He appears in her dreams sometimes, paddling happily in a bathtub or a pothole or curled up, content, on a moist pillow.

A boy in the class says the essay creeps him out.

"In a good way?" Emily asks.

He leans back, two chair legs off the ground. He shrugs.

The drug takes several weeks, sometimes several months, to kick in, and there is still a cluster of red pimples in the crease below Emily's mouth. Her cheeks are pocked with scars and her eyelashes are long and beautiful.

The students don't have much more to say about Emily's essay. It is the best one of the semester, but Brenda doesn't say so.

One Monday after class, there's an email from Sam—longer than usual. Recently, Brenda has been keeping her phone in her desk drawer, because she couldn't stop imagining all the things accumulating in her pocket. Election results and Amber Alerts, pictures of dogs and portentous messages: *Call me* and *Stop by* and *Do you have a min.* Didn't everyone always have a min? This is a temporary fix, at best. While she teaches, the news piles up in the drawer, beside dozens of green pens, waiting for her.

The email says that Sam's sister's baby did not survive. It takes Brenda a while to understand this. She has not, until this moment, known there was a baby in the first place. Her comprehension occurs slowly, as if something unruly is being opened—a box with too many packing peanuts. Brenda pictures Sam's sister's stomach, which was usually firm and tan. She adds a baby to the picture. The stomach becomes firm and tan and round. She takes the baby away.

The email explains that the baby was just a month or two from being born. There was no warning. One morning, Sam's sister woke up with a dull feeling. Like she was a radio that had stopped working, or a phone with a cord—some kind of old machine, plastic that people will soon forget how to use.

In the days afterward, Sam did everything he was told to. By his sister's husband, by the doctor. He bought maxi pads and drinks with lots of electrolytes. He had moved into his own apartment, but he fed his sister's cat and watered her spider plants. Those days, he writes, made him realize he liked being counted on. He stuck a finger in the hanging plant and the soil was moist. He borrowed a ladder. He googled how to throw away lightbulbs. Those days made him realize how much he would like being a dad.

Brenda wishes she had her laptop so that she could snap the screen shut. On the other side of the wall, the professor of modern poetry coughs, and Brenda can hear the mucus in his throat. She is glad for something to be disgusted by. She drags the email into a folder at the edge of her screen, which is labeled *untitled* because she can't bring herself to label it *Sam*.

· · ·

On Halloween, almost half the students arrive in costume: a zombie and an American Girl doll and a lot of cat ears. Emily has fake blood smeared on her cheek and her neck. The red of the blood is the same as the red of her pimples, and it looks as if her face has erupted, as if it has attacked itself.

Brenda has forgotten it's a holiday. The leaves don't change color in this part of the country and pumpkins go soft in the sun. Even if she'd remembered, she wouldn't have known to dress up. Wasn't that for kids? She had never been trick-or-treating herself, because it was one of many things that her father had not allowed: birthday parties and books about wizards and swear words that her students wouldn't even know were swear words.

Instead of a costume, Brenda is wearing the same cardigan she wears every day, the one she keeps in her office all year long to protect against the cold of too much air-conditioning. She believes she gets goose bumps more easily than most people. Her skin contracts in gentle breezes, as if it's afraid of losing its grip on the body underneath.

Casey offers Brenda a plastic crown.

"That's okay," Brenda says. "But thanks."

She looks at her notes. Today's class is supposed to be about revision. At the top of the page, she has written *no one is perfect on the first try*. She rehearses saying this in her head, wondering whether it will sound believable. Everyone is in their seats now, a semicircle of expectant faces, waiting for her to speak. At the beginning of each semester, Brenda requests a classroom with one big table and no desks. In the chair beside her, a boy with pretty eyes and a skinny, stubbly neck removes a set of vampire teeth from his mouth, covered in spit. The girl to his left sucks a lollipop. They seem like children. Of course they will believe her; they believe everything she says.

Brenda puts a prompt on the whiteboard, and the students bend over their notebooks. Surveying the tops of their heads—curly wigs and metallic hair dye, cheap masks pushed off their faces—she is surprised to discover that she feels left out. While they're writing, she slips out of the room and down the hall to the vending machine, where you can buy bags of pretzels crumbled into powder and slices of bright yellow pound cake wrapped in plastic. She has never used the machine, which seems like an artifact of some melancholy past. Half the rows are empty, the labels old and faded.

In the months after her father died, when Brenda was a teenager, she had eaten everything she could get her hands on—the sweeter the better. She ate towering swirls of ice cream, whole sleeves of cookies, sugar dyed purple and pink and blue and poured straight into her mouth. Her friends had long since lost interest in these indulgences—the forbidden thrills they now sought cost more than a few dollars—and so she had been alone with her ravenousness, her tongue raw, her head aching.

Brenda buys all the Skittles left in the machine. Back in the classroom, the students watch while she pours the candy onto a napkin in the middle of the table. It scatters all over, hard rainbow beads in every direction. At least one rolls onto the floor. The students smile politely. *Revision*, Brenda says,

scrawling big, slanted letters on the board. She underlines
vision three times, but they don't write it down. They begin
to believe her just a little bit less.

The candy is still there, untouched, when class ends.
Brenda sits alone at the table and puts a handful in her
mouth. She tries to chew. The sugar coating melts and dribbles down her throat. She watches the students through the
thin rectangular window on the door, their voices far away,
their faces ghost white, blood red, witch green. They look
happy. When Brenda spits the Skittles out, they are wet and
misshapen and all the color is gone.

Brenda buys more candy on the way home from school.
What's left on the shelves is brightly colored or hard to eat—
taffies and big chunks of brittle. She carves a face in an orange
bell pepper, because the pumpkins are sold out. Inside the
trailer, she nibbles the arms and legs off gummy bears and
wonders if her house is considered the haunted house.

The sun goes down and the sidewalk fills up with voices.
Every now and then, they stop—or she thinks they stop—at
the end of the driveway. Brenda arranges the armless gummy
bears in a line. She hears high-pitched voices and low-
pitched voices, children and parents, insisting and resisting.
The gummy bears tumble over, facedown, and she doesn't
pick them up. The hours go by slowly. No one knocks on the
door. The birthday candle inside the pepper has long since
gone out, a hardening puddle of blue wax.

The night turns quiet, as it always does on her street, but
she hears the voices anyway, because they're secret, taunt-

ing sounds. The sound of your hand being taken, the sound of being pulled in the right direction. This house, not this house. The sound of being told where to go.

In the morning, she wakes up too early, early enough to hear the smack of the newspaper landing on pavement.

"I love hearing that," she said to Sam once, while their eyes were still closed. "It's comforting."

"It's suburban," he said.

But she liked it anyway, because it was proof of the kind of life she might one day have: pets and babies, dog walking and gutter cleaning, tying shoes and cleaning knees.

"A boring kind of life," Sam said.

"Only because you've already lived it."

They'd explained their pasts, of course. Brenda got the facts out of the way early, and then she avoided them. They sounded cinematic. They made her feel tired and disorganized, as if her organs had been rearranged, as if all the tubes inside her—for blood and food and air—had taken wrong turns. She drifted in and out of sleep, her head under Sam's chin. She might have said, *Is boring really so bad*, or she might have only dreamed it.

In the middle of the driveway, Brenda finds the newspaper and a carton of eggs with nine left. She isn't wearing shoes or a bra and the sun is rising in brilliant reds and pinks. Three of the eggs are already cracked, leaking orange yolk onto cardboard. There's a roll of soggy toilet paper strung over the branches of the crape myrtle. She pictures teenage boys with puppet arms and untied shoes, with bangs they have to shrug out of their eyes. But it could have been girls, too.

She holds an egg in her palm. The shell is smooth and cold and a little bit wet, covered in the same dew as the newspaper's blue cellophane sleeve. She wonders how hard she would have to press to crush it, to make the whole thing collapse. Her hands look strange, a little monstrous. When she shakes the egg up and down, she can hear the yolk sliding around inside, and that, too, is a strangeness.

When Brenda throws the first egg, it lands in the overgrown flower bed and doesn't break, so she picks it up and throws it harder, against the fence they built to block the view of the neighbors—to block the neighbors' view of them. The egg splatters, then drips. The pieces of the shell are tiny and sharp. She throws the rest one by one while the sun comes up, the sky more and more brilliant, then suddenly grey. She throws them at piles of brick and piles of mud, at Tyvek walls, at the front steps that lead to nowhere. When there are only two left, she takes aim at the aluminum siding of the trailer. The light through the window would look warm and inviting to a stranger.

Brenda cracks the last one in half neatly and watches the phlegmy white slip down the storm drain. She cups the yolk in her palm, careful not to burst the membrane, and throws it as far as she can, into the hole that was once a house. For a moment, it's a gold shape in the air.

NOW YOU KNOW

•

While she followed the recipe on the side of the Wheaties box, my grandmother told me about my grandfather's infidelities. He was in the next room, but he was nearly deaf, and she didn't bother to lower her voice.

"This is important," she said, smashing the cereal with a chicken mallet, until the counter was covered in fine, brown powder.

I was twelve years old, but already it had been decided that I was the keeper of secrets. There were not many good listeners in the family—they liked to yell, even when they weren't angry, as if the volume itself were invigorating—and though in one another they considered silence suspect, in me they considered it a kind of rare treasure. To tell me something, they told themselves, was an investment.

"One day she'll write a book about it," my grandmother said with pride.

"She's the smart kind of quiet," my aunt agreed.

They speculated about whether I would be an artist

or a professor—mysterious, impressive jobs that they knew nothing about. They worried constantly about money, and promised me that by the time I grew up, there wouldn't be anything to worry about.

None of this made sense to me. I kept my secrets to myself—the only reliable way, I thought, to make them disappear. But my relatives believed in a different magic: if their own errors could be the kindling for my success, if an ugly story could become fearsome, undefinable art, then at last it would have nothing to do with them.

My aunt told me about the hitchhiker she had fallen in love with, had never really fallen out of love with. My uncle told me how he got the ugly burns all over his back—he refused to take his shirt off, even in the ocean—and the nightmares he'd had ever since. My cousin, an electrician in Santa Clara, told me how many women he'd seduced while their husbands weren't home, and my other cousin said that *seduction* was a generous word for it. He's our *step*-cousin, the real cousin assured me. My niece, who in our knotted family tree was older than me, called me each time she got a new kind of high.

"Don't ever do what I'm doing," she said.

A few years later, when I was almost sixteen, my grandparents sent me across the country. I had lived with them for as much of my life as I could remember, in the middle of Los Angeles. Our house was small and white, surrounded by plants that had more spikes than leaves. Prickly pear and aloe and the dusty yellow brittlebush. Once a year, the artichoke bloomed, a green grenade turning purple, bursting open to reveal a magenta crown.

It was the same house that my mother had grown up in. When I was ten months old, she'd followed a bird-watcher to South Africa and never returned.

"They were in love," my grandmother said, sometimes incredulously and sometimes mournfully. The bird-watcher was rich—he'd chartered a plane to New Zealand to try to glimpse the famous takahe—but he wasn't my father, whose name no one seemed to know.

A few times a year there were messages from my mother, photos sent to my aunt or uncle, never to me. The turquoise chest of a bee-eater or the unbelievable tail of the sugarbird— twice as long as its body. A penguin rested on its belly, neck outstretched and expectant, like a baby still glued to the ground. My mother herself never appeared in the frame, though sometimes the edge of someone else did: a shoulder, a sneaker, a finger pointing at something we couldn't see. The photos made my grandmother mad or sad, and it was too tiring to predict which; my aunt and uncle had learned to keep them out of sight. But I was considered a willing audience—a necessary one, even.

"You should see this," someone would say, and I never said Why?

The birds were all a little garish, and their strange, excessive beauty seemed like a sort of danger. How could you survive with feathers like that?

One night, after wheeling the trash to the curb, my grandmother returned with news from the neighbors. Luke, the boy across the street, was leaving home. He was fourteen, and already a battery of tests had proven that he was smarter than both his parents. A famous school in Massachusetts saw the tests and said that he could attend for free.

I had known Luke my entire life, but I had hardly ever heard him speak. He wasn't like the other boys on the block, who blared music through open windows and revved the engines of cars they weren't even old enough to drive. Luke looked young—muscleless, an unchiseled chin—but he took linear algebra at the community college, riding his bike back and forth in the evenings, the bag of books on his shoulder tilting him perilously to one side.

My grandparents liked Luke. He was polite and hardworking. But he didn't really belong, and so I could tell they were a little afraid of him, too. They knew what happened, or thought they knew what happened, when people decided they were *going places.* They imagined South Africa, New Zealand, no letters, no phone calls. They knew what the secretary bird looked like—four feet tall, a crown of feathers like exclamation points—but would they recognize their own daughter in a crowd?

So it was a revelation to discover that Luke would be taken away but then sent back—improved and also returned. They believed in the promise of rolling lawns and navy blue uniforms and distinguished alumni. One president plus a few governors, his father bragged while emptying the recycling bin.

When Luke left in September, our street got no louder and no quieter, but each week one of his parents appeared with the trash can and good news. The food was excellent. The teachers were strict. Luke's roommate had met the Poet

Laureate. (My grandparents had never heard of the Poet Laureate.) By October, it was decided that I should leave, too. I took a many-hour test at a school on the other side of the Hollywood Hills. Halfway through, the girl in front of me vomited, splattering my shoes. A few people stared, then turned back to their multiple choice, noses plugged. Eventually, someone guided her out of the room, and part of me envied her escape.

In the end, there was no space at the school in Massachusetts, or maybe no money, and so my grandmother found a school in Vermont instead. A glossy brochure promised mountains that turned orange and red every year. I wasn't interested in leaving home, but I knew that resistance would be unsurprising, and I wanted no part in teenage fury. When my aunts and uncles took up fury on my behalf—you're *sending* her away?—I became even more compliant. Among the school's graduates, my grandmother assured me, there were a few CEOs and a famous flautist.

"A flautist?" I asked.

"An artist," she said, smiling expectantly, waiting for me to share her delight. "You love art."

Vermont was a place I had considered on the map only because of the way it was wedged next to New Hampshire, a ragged-edged lover with no way to the water. I lived in a red-brick dormitory, in which the bedrooms, like many of the classrooms, had ornate fireplaces you weren't allowed to use. My roommate was summoned home after two weeks— her father's indictment appeared in the newspapers—and so

I lived alone. The classes were all too difficult. I took algebra while everyone else took geometry. I encountered Old
English, which didn't sound anything like real English.

In the field behind the headmaster's house—white
columns, a garage that hid an unknown number of cars—
there was a farm, or what we called a farm: a chicken coop,
a lettuce patch and an herb garden, a pregnant mare. The
headmaster himself was a history teacher who'd once been
a lawyer, but his wife believed, above all, in nature. She gar-
dened in her husband's old dress shirts and said that some
things had to be learned in the mud. She also taught ecol-
ogy, which soon became my favorite subject: the creeping
retreat of glaciers, the universe contained in one palmful
of soil. The world, she told us, was not a globe but a web.
Everyone in the class was assigned a small plot of land, no
bigger than my grandmother's kitchen, in the forest beyond
the tennis courts. Not to own or even to tend, but just to
know, backwards and forwards. As if it were your home, she
said—because it is.

There were boys and girls at the school but there were
more boys. I disliked competition, so I ignored it. In the
afternoons, when classes were over, I retreated to my piece of
land, walking its imaginary perimeter again and again, until
the sound of twigs and leaves under my boots was unbearable, like too-loud chewing, and then I sat still, shivering, to
give the silence its due. On one of the last days before the
clocks turned back, I was sitting there hugging myself, when
a girl I'd never spoken to appeared at the edge of my plot. She
was tall and skinny and her face was crowded with freckles.
She leaned against an oak tree, which I had determined—

unscientifically—to be the oldest tree in sight. Its bark was thick and cracked like a topographical map.

"Hey," I said, holding my knees. "Get off my land."

The girl smiled. She turned her face into the bark and tilted her chin, so that she was looking straight up the trunk. She stood there for a few seconds, and then she did—she got off my land. She had bright red hair that I watched disappear through the trees.

For the rest of the afternoon, I made myself busy, raking leaves into a pile in the center of my plot, sorting small sticks and big sticks and four heavy logs, which I used to mark the land's borders. Dirt floor, wood walls. It became a clean square in the forest, a space to fill in. And when I left, I stopped at the tree and put my chin where her chin had been. I gazed up as far as I could: empty branches, grey sky, so many fingers grasping at air.

The next day, I walked around the square but I didn't go inside it. I waited for her. The day after that, a colt was born. The headmaster's wife made the announcement in the morning, and after breakfast we all leaned against the fence and watched it run its first wobbly circles. Its legs were slick with blood and looked snappable. A boy with white hair and white eyelashes—he wore sunglasses most of the time, even in the shade—said it looked afraid, and everyone agreed.

On the third day, she was standing in the middle of the square when I arrived. New leaves had fallen, bright ones, not yet brown and dry or brown and wet, and I picked them up one at a time as I approached.

Her name was Madeleine. I already knew so I never asked. She touched my body like it was a door to someplace, pushing and pulling, holding me—I had never been held— but also trying to get past me, to whatever it was that was there on the other side. She put her mouth around my breasts and in my armpits and at last between my legs. She took her shirt off and kept her pants on. When she pulled away, sud- denly, she crouched on the ground, her face scrunched up in an expression I couldn't read—like a child's face, full of the pain of an unknown resolve.

We sat there for a while, leaning against the neat stacks of wood, the dirt cold and exposed. Whatever it was that I had been preparing for seemed suddenly laughable— unbelievable. But she was the one to laugh. A rough, unyield- ing laugh that had nothing to do with the sound of her voice, or the sound I had heard at the back of her throat—a sort of gurgling, as if pleasure were something liquid inside her.

I stayed in the woods until the sun went down and three of my fingers lost all their color. I thought about the colt and the mare and the white eyelashes and the freckles all over Madeleine's face. I recited these things, memorized them, because it seemed to me that one day I would need them. Baby, mother, boy, girl. Blood, hair, skin. Or perhaps it only seemed this way because they were slipping away--an orange head receding through the trees, a horse already smooth and steady on its feet, already unremarkable.

When I returned home that summer, I told my grand- mother there was nothing left to learn in Vermont. She didn't fight back, but she made me tell her about the seasons. She invited my aunt and uncle for dinner, and I told them how the trees had seemed most alive to me in the winter. The branches encased in ice made me think of what was trapped inside, the current of something—I pictured veins— keeping it warm. Sometimes, I told them, the weight of the snow bent the trees until they almost touched the ground. They reared up if you shook them free, like the ecstatic loosing of water off a dog's back.

"What about the fall?" my aunt wanted to know.

"All those colors," my grandmother said.

I hesitated. They didn't know as little as they pretended. The hills around us turned yellow every year, the grass crumbling between your fingertips. There was frost some mornings and occasionally the biblical assault of hail. They had seen snow in the mountains.

I shrugged.

"Don't be selfish," my aunt said.

For a few weeks, my friends from school called. They lived in New York and New Jersey and sometimes the calls came while we were still asleep. My grandmother answered in a fog. She brought me the phone in bed and watched from the doorway while I talked. Her hair, which she coiled into a tight bun every morning, hung over her shoulder in a single thin braid, like a snake. The conversations were halting. I pictured my friends in big backyards—electric green grass, golden dogs—or else on golf courses.

"Next time," I told my grandmother, "tell them I'm not home."

"You're always home," she said.

"Say I'm unavailable."

She narrowed her eyes.

"Is that the truth?"

I nodded. I spent the summer biking and drawing and slowly beginning to paint, because these were things I could do alone. The paintings reassured my grandmother, who bought me acrylics and then oils, a wooden palette and paintbrushes made from weasels' tails. I woke up early, while it was cool and bugless, before the neighbor's radio turned on. In the afternoon, I spread the canvases all over the concrete yard to dry in the sun. I liked to go up to the roof and look down on them all like that, square after square of color, the flaws made small, almost invisible, from a distance.

I decided to paint a portrait of everyone I knew. Some of them came to sit for me, because it seemed like an old-fashioned sort of honor. My uncle's face, sweating with the effort of keeping still. My niece's perfectly—unnervingly—frozen smile. My grandmother folded her hands in her lap and my grandfather kept scratching behind his ear. Others I painted from memory: the neighbor with the leaf blower, the cook from Vermont, the drama teacher at the school I was going back to. I sketched the girl at the smoothie place, whose hair hung in front of her face when she leaned over the blenders, hiding the ruby stud in her nostril. When I ran out of canvases, I crowded faces into the frame, cousins peering over each other's shoulders, Luke's face beside the profile of the boy on the corner, the one who'd gone to prison for holding someone else's gun. And when I was done, I propped the canvases against the fence in the yard and we called it a show. My grandmother walked through slowly, standing for minutes in front of each painting, brow furrowed in her best performance of discernment. My grandfather was efficient. He looked one by one, sometimes leaning close—"Is this *black* or *brown?*"—and then he sat down in a plastic lawn chair, folded his glasses, and said, "Well, they all look just like you."

My grandmother turned around.

"That's it!" she said. "I knew there was something."

"Something?" I asked.

"All the eyes are your eyes."

I stopped painting people after that, because I didn't want to be surprised by my own face. My grandparents didn't understand what had gone wrong. I filled a huge sheet of paper with grey squares and slightly less-grey squares. They looked at each other, worried.

"Why don't you go to the movies?" my grandmother said.

"Why don't you get an ice cream?" my grandfather said.

I understood this to mean *Why don't you get a boyfriend,* and so I ate cone after cone by myself, in something like defiance, until my stomach ached. The ice cream melted all over my fingers. I wiped my hands on my shorts.

Once, late at night, I filled a water glass with Scotch. My grandmother kept the liquor under the sink, beside the cleaning supplies, because my mother had liked to drink. *Poison,* I was told. The Scotch was a grudging concession to my grandfather, who insisted on a splash over ice at the end of a meal. I drank until everything seemed muffled. It was a lonely experiment—the sound of my own footsteps shuffling at the other end of the hall—and I didn't try it again.

. . .

When I graduated from high school, my grandparents did what they could to get me to go to college. They used all the usual metaphors to describe my future: open doors, bright lights. They couldn't afford tuition, but they promised other purchases anyway. A car, a computer, a minifridge, whatever it was a student needed. I declined all this politely, and then not so politely. I said the things I had heard my classmates say—school was boring, school was pointless— even though what I really meant was that school was unkind.

At the beginning of September, I hitched a ride to San Francisco. Our next-door neighbor, Tina, was driving all the way for the sake of a kitten. Tina was twice my age, but she didn't look it. She wore torn jean shorts and painted streaks of electric color above her eyes. She'd been disappointed by life, my grandmother said, though none of us ever knew why. I told my grandmother that I would stay in San Francisco for a month, maybe two, that I'd be back, but she didn't believe me. The first time my mother ran away, as a teenager, she wound up there, sleeping along the water.

"She took a tent to the Embarcadero," my aunt said. "Eventually she met some guy with an RV. He kept a llama as a pet."

"No, no," my grandmother said. "He had a real house."

Her voice was cold, metallic. It was hard to tell whether she was defending my mother or accusing her.

While we drove, Tina listened to a call-in show on the radio and chewed one stick of gum after another. The car smelled like cinnamon. The callers asked for advice about snoring husbands and cheating husbands, husbands who had lost themselves at the office or on the Internet, husbands whose second lives had been revealed like cockroaches writhing in the kitchen light. The host of the show was a woman who murmured in all the right places. She didn't promise that the men would be changed or restored or even punished.

"Now you know," she said, her voice smooth and mild.

The woman with the kitten lived at the top of a hill so steep the cars had bricks behind their wheels. Her house was all one color. The walls, the door, the window frames, the flower boxes attached to the window frames were all a single bright blue, a cloak tossed over the whole thing. And so when the woman opened the door, it seemed like she was emerging from under something—like she was uncovering herself. Black hair, white shirt, eyes the color of sand in the sun. She held the cat against her chest.

"Helen?" Tina said.

"That's me." She sounded surprised, or maybe just delighted, as if she had discovered she was wearing socks that didn't quite match.

The kitten opened her eyes in alarm when Helen held her out. But then Tina cradled her against her chest— another warm, indistinguishable beat—and the kitten closed her eyes again.

Helen invited us inside, which was how I found out she was a painter, the first painter I had ever known. Half the house was for working, covered in drop cloths that were covered in color, old and new. There were drawings taped all over the walls and masking tape where other drawings had once been, beige edges bringing a white square into existence.

It was hard to tell how old Helen was. She might have been about thirty—closer to Tina's age than mine—but there was something childlike, haphazard about her. She told us she'd been in art school for a few years, but she'd dropped out just a few months short of finishing. There was one strand of white in her hair, tucked behind her ear.

"Have you named her?" Tina said, changing the subject.

"I never name them."

Tina nodded sympathetically. "No use getting attached."

"Oh no, even the ones I keep. They're nameless, too."

Tina gave her a blank look.

"I just can't presume to know," Helen said. She smiled sheepishly at me. "It sounds weird."

I shook my head but didn't say anything. I admired principles like these—it didn't seem to me that I had any of my own—but I worried that admiration would make me sound stupid.

While they talked about the cat, I wandered all over the house. The walls were crowded but there wasn't much furniture. One brown velvet couch, wide enough for sleeping, and otherwise wood: bar stools and footstools, a coffee table with an oblong knot in the middle, a leaky eye staring out at me. Her paintings were all big paintings—nearly as tall as me and sometimes just as wide. The paint itself was thick, forming ridges and waves and globs on the surface. If you looked closely, there was stuff in it, or underneath it: sand mixed in to make a grainy white, leaves and scraps of paper

flattened by swipes of grey green. In one, you could make
out the shape of an envelope and the crenellated edges of a
Forever stamp.

The only room without paintings was the room for the
kittens. Four still left. I sat down, letting them climb over
me, because it was easier to think there, the empty walls and
the warm animals, the shameless desperation of their claws
on my clothes. When Helen opened the door, I stood up and
the kittens held on, clinging to the hem of my shirt. Tina
appeared behind her.

"Where to next?" she asked, sounding a little impatient.

The kitten scrabbled down one of my legs.

"Oh." I had vague plans. The friend of a friend. A pull-
out couch.

The address was written on a scrap of paper. Helen
explained that it was across the Bay, which was how she
ended up telling Tina to leave and me to stay. When rush
hour was over, she promised she'd drive me herself.

When Tina was gone, Helen made two glasses of juice
from a machine with a lot of parts. There was an enormous
skylight in the kitchen, and the room was several degrees
warmer than the rest of the house. She fed a whole apple
into the machine. The juice was grainy and beige, nothing
like the clear stuff from the store.

"The stuff that looks like piss," Helen said.

We drank quietly, bits of fruit clinging to the sides of the
glasses, and then I said, "I'd like to be a painter." I didn't say
too.

Helen frowned. "You make it sound like a confession."

"Maybe it is."

She was standing in the middle of the light, sweat beading above her lip.

"Well, how do you feel now?" she said. "Unburdened?"

She told me she was from Texas, a smallish city where almost everybody believed in God. Her parents weren't religious, but they were doctors; they, too, had made a business out of saving people. She'd rejected all that. At first, she thought she wanted to be a ceramicist, maybe even a sculptor, because she liked building stuff, and she even liked destroying stuff, especially if it meant getting back the parts you started with—a twisted heap of mud on the wheel. Even now, what she liked best about paint was its texture.

"Do your parents wish you were a savior?" I asked.

She had turned away from me and was looking out the window at the small, overgrown yard.

"You can be a painter," Helen said. Outside, the kittens' mother stalked back and forth in front of a row of ferns. "You can be one right now. You don't have to wait for someone else to tell you."

I started to say something, then stopped. Helen turned back to face me. The dust was suspended—beautiful—in the light between us.

"I know," she said, and smiled.

When I was on the other side of the city—folding and unfolding the couch like an arthritic skeleton, imagining the bridge, the water, the steep streets between that couch and her couch—I heard her say this again and again. What was there to know? I pictured Helen standing in my grandparents' yard, surrounded by all my canvases, staring at a dozen

unfamiliar faces, a dozen pairs of my own eyes. I made a
list of everything I wanted her to know and would never be
able to explain: my mother, my grandmother, someone else's
bare chest in the middle of a forest. I had tried to make a
sculpture once, before giving up—a rough clay shape made
and remade until the heat of my fingers turned it soft and
unusable.

I spent a few obligatory nights with my spine against the
couch's spine, and then I took three buses back the way I had
come. I walked all the way up the hill, the cars tilted toward
me, straining to be released. When she opened the door, her
arms empty this time, the broken remains of concentration
on her face, I wanted to ask: Did you know *this*? Did you
know I'd be back?

I stayed in San Francisco for a year. My grandmother
said *I told you so*, and I let her have the pleasure of being
right. A small, cruel pleasure, like the last acid mouthfuls of
a bottle of wine you didn't mean to drink. I told her I was
living with a friend.

I painted more than ever—my colors next to Helen's, on
the wall, on the floor, on the rough tips of our fingers. We
called the cat *sweetie* or *baby* or *your highness*. There was
one more litter and four more strangers who came to take
them away, happy to put their anonymous heartbeats to use.
Eventually, I got a job gardening. The man I worked for was
a landscape architect, who wore tucked-in shirts and shoes
that didn't get dirty. I mulched and weeded. I pulled tent
caterpillars' webs from trees—thick, white shrouds, like Hal-

loween decorations left out in the rain. I learned the names of flowers and the names of flower colors: salsa red, infrared apricot, elfin white.

I worked in the early mornings, when everything was draped in mist, and sometimes Helen worked all night. I painted less and less. I was tired by the time I came home, and shrank away from Helen's energy. She ate ginseng root and M&M's by the fistful. She lay on the ground, her hair fanned out like a peacock's tail, and told me one idea after another. Sometimes she asked me what I was working on and my mind went blank, or else it lit up—not with thoughts so much as flashes, the unnameable color of possibilities— and there was nothing I could do but watch. When I went to sleep, I was relieved not to dream.

Her show opened on a rainy Friday. I bought a cowl-neck dress for the occasion. Helen laughed and wore a T-shirt. An almost-important critic stood in front of a painting called *Self-Portrait*, his lips pursed. There were never any figures in Helen's work, but sometimes I saw them there anyway: the whirl of an ear, the web of interlocking hands.

The next summer, when she had sold two paintings and thought she might be about to sell a third, Helen announced we were going to Italy. Anyone who loves art, she said, needs to see Rome. She didn't call me an artist, I thought, because by then I wasn't one.

I had never been outside the country. At the airport, the security line snaked back and forth for nearly an hour. The woman behind us suddenly doubled over in pain, moaning cinematically, and was whisked straight to the front. I wondered if she was performing, then wished I had a performance in me.

Helen saw the man while I was bent over, untying my shoes. He was inside the body scanner, arms outstretched, in socks. When I stood up, they were already staring at each other. He was older than Helen, his hair cut close to his skull and beginning to grey in places, but he was tall and muscular, with posture good enough to notice. He might have been a dancer. Helen raised her hand and held it there, not waving. The machine rotated back and forth around the man. He dropped his arms sooner than he should have, then lifted them back up again. His mouth said sorry to someone we couldn't see.

He waited for us on the other side of security, his belt back on, checking his watch.

"It sounds like an excuse," he said, "but I really do have a plane to catch."

There was a long pause, in which Helen didn't introduce me. The man told Helen he'd seen the latest reviews. He didn't say *congratulations*, but Helen said *thanks*. She had her hand on her throat and her shoes were untied, their tongues loose.

I had never heard of the man, but after that I learned all about him. They had been in love for years. He was the one who found the house—bought the house—and he was the one who painted it blue. He was a playwright who won prizes and was always flying to New York. At one point, he had been designated a genius.

"What do you mean, designated?" I said.

"Never mind," Helen said.

Neither of them had believed in pets. They liked animals—revered them even—but they couldn't wrap their heads around domestication. There was a mangy tiger cat who loitered around the back door, and one day she deposited three babies at the base of the gutter. They drove to the pet store, the litter swaddled in Helen's T-shirt. Just a week later, the man left for good, and the first thing Helen did was go back to the store. There was one kitten left.

Rome was hot, and my body clung to me. In the heat, we ate too little and drank too much. We fought. We stayed up as late as we could, since the nights were cooler, which was how we came to know the city's feral cats. They were everywhere, and it was impossible for me to separate their presence from the man's presence, as if it were him slinking around corners, approaching then retreating, curious then indifferent.

I had a cheap, bulky camera with me that I kept forgetting to use. One night, while we were sitting outside a restaurant, at a table with three legs on the ground, an elongated shadow appeared on the wall beside us, a cat's back arched cartoonishly. We were close enough that we could see the individual hairs in the shadow. I got out of my chair and crouched with my camera.

"What are you doing?" Helen said, her voice impatient, sharp.

I didn't respond. I pointed the camera at the shadow, then slowly turned to face the cat. It paused for a moment to meet my gaze and darted into the street—long legs, gnawed ear, a reptilian hiss.

"What are you doing?" She sounded desperate now, and something about her desperation liberated me. I took one picture after another. The cat flicked its tail regally.

When I returned to the table, the bottle of wine was empty and the check had been paid.

"That's going to be a terrible picture."

San Francisco was drizzly and foreboding when we came back. Within a month, I flew home to Los Angeles. Helen bought the ticket. For the first time in my life, I called a taxi, even though she'd offered to drive me to the airport. Waiting for it at the bottom of the hill, I thought about leaning my easel against the mailbox and abandoning it there. There would have been some satisfaction, I thought, in a dramatic renunciation. In the end, practical considerations prevailed—it wasn't cheap, what would my grandmother say—and this seemed like a failure of will, proof of just how little my life resembled my image of it. Here were the materials, now where was the composition?

I had hoped I might forget about the roll of film. I imagined discovering it years later, when I could no longer remember what it was—what I had been trying to capture. The past would be astonishing that way, glossy and new. Instead, I thought about the photographs all the time. The man who developed them was apologetic. Helen had been right: they were terrible. One grey blur on top of another. The cat rarely sat still, but when it did, it looked straight at me, its eyes glowing huge and yellow.

. . .

Two years later, Helen's paintings came to Los Angeles. A new show, her biggest yet. My grandfather had died, and I had moved back into my grandmother's house. We pretended this was a favor to me: the city was changing, the rents were hard to believe. The truth was that she needed help. She lived on the ground floor to avoid the stairs and coughed noisily for much of the night. The sound kept me up, but so did the silence.

I had another gardening job, slightly better than the first. My grandmother didn't like the dirt on my knees and under my fingernails, but she was pleased, too. She told my aunt I was rising through the ranks. I worked for as many hours as I could, as long as it was light out, planting tall grasses and low shrubs on whatever land the city owned: parks, medians, the huge concrete planters outside municipal buildings. The idea was to grow only native plants, to save water and money, to save bees and butterflies. When I got home, my grandmother was always waiting for me. I never asked what she did all day, because I was afraid the answer was nothing. She watched me eat and told me stories she thought I'd never heard.

"Your uncle," she said, sounding conspiratorial, "is color-blind."

"That's not a secret, Nana."

This offended her.

"Well, it isn't good."

Her eyes went distant. She rubbed the tablecloth—red

and yellow flowers, vivid green vines—between her thumb and her index finger.

"I may be dying," she said, "but I can still see colors."

"You're not dying, Nana."

Her eyes returned. She looked at me.

"We're all dying."

I took her to see the paintings just before they came down, when I could be sure Helen wouldn't be there. I told my grandmother the artist was someone I knew a little—from afar.

"Helen," she said, reading the name painted on the wall. She said it with the same kind of amazement Helen did when she came face-to-face with something unknown. In all those months, had she ever heard that wonder in my voice? Part of me, the part that was afraid, hoped that she hadn't.

I had prepared myself for what I might see at the show, which I thought might protect me from the assault of recognition. Of course, it didn't. I recognized the paintings and it seemed as if they recognized me. We stared at one another across the room and I tried to feel triumphant: the paintings, at least, couldn't turn away.

The paint was dense and complicated. The reviews, which I had read one by one, made much of this. "Paint so thick it becomes an object." "Indeed, the paint *contains* objects." They wondered aloud what all this meant.

"What's in here?" my grandmother said, leaning forward. "It looks like hair."

She was looking at the corner of a large reddish painting. She was right. Under thick globs of crimson, there was

a tangle of hair, like what you leave behind in the shower.
Nearby there was a spray of shorter hairs—flyaways—and a
ball of coiled pubic hairs. There were delicate strands that
might have been eyelashes. In the center of the canvas, there
was a pile of toenails.

"Interesting," my grandmother said.

The toenails belonged to me. One morning, Helen had
looked at my feet hanging over the end of the bed and asked
if she could have them: ten half-moons. She cradled my foot
in her lap and clipped. She laughed.

I had watched her coat the nails with color. Cadmium
red, alizarin crimson, burnt sienna. But standing in front of
the painting—*Do not touch,* the signs said—I began to doubt
that they were really mine. They looked like anyone else's. A
woman's, a man's. I wondered which parts of myself I would
recognize for sure, which parts I could pick out of a crowd.

The truth is that the paintings were even thicker than
the critics suspected. Under each painting there was another
one, sometimes two, even three. They were bad paintings—
Helen said so—from old phases, covered up with a solid color
so that she could begin again. It wasn't such an unusual way
to work; lots of artists, the not-famous ones, saved money this
way. So it was a kind of good fortune, she told me, to have
paintings you disliked, or disavowed.

My grandmother wandered slowly around the room,
stomping her foot every now and then, which she said she
had to do to keep it awake. She stopped in front of the best
painting in the room. Huge and blue and hard to look at up
close. Helen's best painting, which contained three more of
her worst. I could remember the third, the one just below the

surface, but I had no idea what the first and the second ones looked like—perhaps I'd never seen them. Helen said she herself often forgot, and there was no way to find out. The layers couldn't be peeled back, the way wallpaper can be.

I imagined chipping away at it, flaking off colors in pieces that might or might not jog our memory. Mine, hers. Eventually we'd glimpse the canvas. A little bit of not-quite white, like hitting bone. But I don't think we'd want to see that. I think we'd stop once we'd seen that.

SEPARATION

·

He asked her out at the reservoir, where she went skinny-dipping in the summer. Early in the morning, before all the kids arrived, or sometimes late at night, when all the sounds of the water seemed louder: lapping, splashing, frogs. She was toweling her hair when he appeared, and she wasn't wearing any pants. Her pubic hair was unkempt.

Kate was taken aback, but she said yes. As he walked away, she noticed his uncertain footing on the rocks and the spray of eczema, like something coughed up, trailing down his back and into his bathing suit. Already she had forgotten his name.

When she arrived at the restaurant—white tablecloths, heavy menus, a basket of bread swaddled to keep warm—he was wearing enormous glasses. He stood up and his napkin fell out of his lap. If you looked at the glasses from the side, you could see just how thick the lenses were—opaque, like a frosted shower door. His name was Nick, and when they undressed in her bedroom that night, his hands darting all over her skin, she felt certain that he was seeing her for the first time.

In two years, they were married. The story of the pants—the pantslessness—had become well known. Predictably, it featured in several wedding toasts. The glasses were removed to demonstrate. He really can't see! Nick smiled good-naturedly, pawing the air hopelessly to make them all laugh. The eczema crawled out from under his white collar.

Someone drove them home, and at the last minute Nick said to turn the car around. He checked them into a hotel, a cheap one, and they rode the elevator laughing. They had sex in overstarched sheets. They had agreed they didn't believe in honeymoons.

"So what's all this," Kate said, smiling. She waved at the plastic nightstand painted like wood. The warping watercolor above the headboard, a flimsy French lake.

"Well," he said. His beliefs had been ill-advised.

He kept the glasses on as long as he could. She kissed him. Her pubic hair was more kempt than it used to be. He tasted her.

"You don't need those," she said, taking the glasses off. "You know me."

"I do."

In two years they were married and in three years he was dead. They didn't have the chance to make rash decisions. By the time they might have considered a house, idling the engine in unaffordable neighborhoods, spinning fantasies and squandering savings, they were already carrying around the diagnosis. Kate imagined it on a little slip of paper—in pockets and purses, in the glove compartment during long drives, in the cluttered kitchen drawer where they kept cheap, indispensable things. They never forgot where it was. They kept the medical bills in a pile on the bedside table, and when there was nothing to do but wait, Kate stacked and restacked them, pushing the edges into alignment. The bills were big and hard to decipher. Numbers they had to look up, which were codes for words they also had to look up.

They said, "Let's do some math."

They never said, "Let's plan ahead."

They found one bedroom and one and a half baths near the hospital, with pink trim and pink cabinet doors that hung off their hinges like limbs.

Everyone talked about fighting, being a fighter.

"For newlyweds, we do an awful lot of fighting," Nick said while they waited for the doctor to be right with them.

There was time, in the end, for him to make his own arrangements.

"No speeches, of course."

"Of course?"

"Just put some snacks out," he said. "Pigs in blankets."

"That's ridiculous," Kate said.

"And Pringles."

"Don't you have a favorite poem?"

"You can make it a joke," Nick said. "A joke will be a relief."

Kate did what he asked, because she wanted it to be exactly as he had pictured it. He had been afraid—when he admitted to being afraid—of the size of the future, of his own desperate predictions, of the simple question that only time would tell, but not to him: now what?

She chopped the hot dogs and wrapped them in dough from a canister, the kind that twisted and popped, jolting her each time, even though the large print on the label told her what to expect. She piled them in pyramids and put platters everywhere. She overdid it. On the pink mantel and above the cabinets. In the hall, for people waiting to use the half bath. She took bowls of chips from one person to the next, raw faces whose tears seemed to have nothing to do with her. They offered to help, but Kate held the serving dishes tightly against her chest. And when they were gone, when the pyramids were still mostly intact, she sat down and cried over his joke.

What happened next wasn't that she recovered—never that, really—but she did move to a new city, where she would have to bump into life every day. She got a job at a nursery school. She rented an attic room with a slanted turquoise ceiling. On weekends, she woke to the sound of things being banged in the house's shared kitchen. Old muffled sounds, which she heard and remembered all at once. Kate lingered like that, her eyelids erupting with morning color.

The children at the school where she worked were undergoing separation. A technical term—to be left on one's own. It involved several steps, which could not be skipped or performed out of sequence.

First, the mothers left the room for five minutes. This was just practice. They timed the minutes on their dangly watches and returned as soon as the second hand permitted.

"Ta-da," they said, waiting to see relief mirrored on their children's faces.

Next, the mothers said good-bye in earnest. Kate told them to wait in the hallway—in case. Sometimes children drifted out the door, crawling beside dump trucks or steering shopping carts of plastic produce, and were surprised to find the mothers hiding, towering over miniature chairs in primary colors. They drove their trucks into the high heels or sensible flats blocking their way.

"Beep beep," they said.

"Move," they said.

Kate worked at the nursery school for too many years. The women she worked with had grey or orange hair and arms that jiggled when they scrubbed the tabletops. Kate wondered if she really belonged there. Her stomach sunk between her hips, muscles showed through her skin. She didn't think this looked attractive. She thought it looked a little grotesque.

Each year, Kate separated a new group of children. Some of the mothers envied her stomach and her throaty neck, her bare face a reproach to theirs, which were painted gold and pink with time they didn't have. There were occasions, Kate thought, when they despised her. When their clothes were no longer clung to, when they entered the classroom and no one looked up. Or all the times in between, at a desk or a sink or a jammed-up intersection, when their children surged back into awareness, when the mothers realized— a crest of guilt and fear—how long they had managed to forget them.

At the end of every day, Kate stood by herself in the cen-

ter of the carpet, a checkerboard of loud colors. She held out
the implausibly small knapsacks. One year, there was a father
among the mothers. His face was big, nearly ugly. But he was
tall and tanned and his voice was so softly beautiful that Kate
let herself assume it was full of the same grief as hers.

When she looked at his tongue on her skin, she didn't
believe her own body. When she lowered herself onto him,
she wished she had dimples at the base of her back, hips
with flesh he could hold on to. He cooked her cream sauces
and meat sauces, bought expensive, oozing cheeses. For one
month, she had sex with him and hoped to change shape.
He told her she was warm inside, and she shook her head,
unconvinced.

"Touch yourself."

He propped himself up on his elbow and watched.
Kate slid her index finger inside her vagina. It was slick and
smooth, except where it was rough. Were there any other
muscles you could touch? It seemed as if the walls of her
body were closing in around her finger. It had never occurred
to her that she had walls.

Then one afternoon, while the classroom emptied, she
held out the knapsack for the man's son. She was weaving
his arms through the straps when she heard a woman's voice
calling his name, high and kind and careless. Kate walked
outside beside them. She stood in the parking lot, waving at
her reflection in the mother's car window.

Kate up and left. Years later, she still repeated this phrase,
she liked it so much. That *up* could be a verb! A house lifted

right off its foundation. She pictured the moment when the whole clapboard thing hovered over its footprint, casting a shadow on the dirt.

She went to work in a cubicle where she answered two different phones and took notes on many pads. Sometimes she unplugged the phones and listened to the bleating rings and disembodied scribbling on the other side of the grey particleboard. According to company policy, the phones rang exactly one and a half times. It was boring; it delighted her.

The women in the office wore belted dresses and tortoiseshell hair clips. They enjoyed setting Kate up on dates. The men all had dependable jobs, possibly in cubicles of their own or sometimes, as they made known, in offices with multiple windows.

She was on a date with a man who had two windows when she met her second husband. They were both waiting for change, their drinks sweating in their hands. Kate saw him in the mirror behind the bar, where his face hovered above two bottles of gin. In the other corner of the mirror, beside the liqueurs, she saw the back of her date's head.

"Can you make eye contact in a mirror?" the man above the gin said.

"What?" She picked up the bills from the counter.

"If I'm looking at you from across the room," he said, "and you're looking at me. We both know we're looking."

"Ah," she said, "but if I'm looking at you in the mirror, and you're looking at me in the mirror—"

"Yes," they said at the same time.

.   .   .

When Kate and Felix's daughter was old enough to start nursery school, Kate put her foot down. Leah was three. She had fine yellow hair—Felix's hair—and too many teeth in her mouth.

"Not yet," Kate said.

Felix called several schools. He found one with an enlightened pedagogy and baby rabbits in the classrooms. There were no reptiles. Leah hated reptiles.

"She's ready," he said.

"Don't use the script on me," Kate shouted. "I *wrote* the script."

In general, she didn't shout.

"Next year," she said, more gently. "Can one more year really hurt?"

Leah wrapped herself around Felix's leg. He lifted her above his head and made her laugh. She kicked her feet, pretending to be afraid, hitting him in the chest, then in the nose.

"Be careful," Kate said, while Felix raised Leah even higher.

"It's all right. It's nothing."

Kate went upstairs. She sat at her desk, listening to them laugh. She gave herself tasks—untangled a pile of paper clips, tested her pens for ink. The desk was filled with pictures and postcards and other scraps. Mostly, they were scraps of Nick. A matchbook, a receipt with his signature, a Post-it note from the fridge: *Need more ketchup.* Every year she promised herself she would go through it all. She called them *remnants* once, but the drama of the word embarrassed her.

Someday—soon—she'd take it all up to the attic, because

this was how she had arranged the story in the version she liked best. Leah, long and lean, with fewer teeth, would be upstairs, sliding boxes, banging knees and elbows in the crawl space. Two floors below, Kate would close her eyes and wait for the moment when her daughter would emerge, filmed with dust, radiant with her question: who is *this*?

Kate's story never happened. She labeled and stacked the boxes in the attic, but no one ever went up there, and anyway, Leah didn't like photo albums. She'd taken a photography class for a few weeks, but couldn't get used to the camera—all its cruel sounds. Clicks and flashes, the menacing zoom. Whenever she saw a picture of herself, she winced.

When Leah turned fifteen, she began starving herself. This was the sort of thing, Kate knew, that teenage girls did, but she had imagined it differently. She'd imagined vain girls or boring girls, girls with boyfriends and sparkly makeup. Or maybe sad girls, girls with bad parents, secret abortions—things that swallowed them up. Leah's life was smooth and unblemished.

It took them months to notice. By then Leah's clothes were all too big, and she was always cold. Kate wondered how they could have been so stupid.

"What if we'd caught it earlier?" she said to Felix.

There was hair all over Leah's body, which the doctor had a special name for. It was the same hair that newborns had. Soft and colorless, the kind that looks, in the right light, like the glow of a halo. Once the doctors were involved, the rules were strict. Five meals a day, thick and white: whole milk and real butter, yogurt with cream on top. Leah had to quit the swim team and then the track team. When Felix found her doing sit-ups in the middle of the night, Kate called the nutritionist's cell phone.

"Eat a big breakfast," he suggested.

"Like what?"

"Well." The nutritionist sounded groggy. "How about a bagel with cream cheese?"

The rules made Leah cry. She'd followed all the others, hadn't she? No drugs, no sex, no driving without a license.

"This isn't punishment," Kate said.

Leah stared at the bagel. She licked her finger and ate the sesame seeds one at a time.

"Don't rush me." Tears dribbled into her mouth.

"We've got time," Felix said. "All the time in the world."

Kate didn't really believe him. She followed the rules, too, out of something like penance. Potato chips at lunch, ice cream just hours before dinner. Her coffee came with skim milk—watery, almost blue—and she sent it back. She weighed herself every day, because she wanted to see the numbers grow. But nothing changed. If anything, her skin got cleaner, her hair got shinier.

One afternoon, Kate came home early and found Leah in the bathroom, blood running down her leg and all over her foot. She was standing in the tub, the water turning pink. Kate knew about mothers who did heroic things with the help of adrenaline—vaulted over fences, jumped into the ocean. And so when she sprang into action, when she felt the panicked hum in her temples and the muscly confusion

in her throat, she told herself that this was how rescue stories were supposed to go. When she found herself kneeling
beside the tub, holding her daughter's shin in her hands,
what she said was "Who did this to you?"

"What?"

Kate looked up at Leah, who seemed so tall and calm—
almost a stranger.

"I'm fine."

Up close, Kate could see that the cut was small. She
let go and there was blood on her fingers. *Collect yourself,*
she said in her head, because it was something to visualize: a rewound video of broken glass, all the pieces reassem-
bling themselves into a single, seamless shape. When she
spoke again, her voice was her teacher voice. She found the
paper towels and the Band-Aids, she squeezed the very last
of the Neosporin from the tube. Leah sat down in the tub
in her underwear, her socks draped over the edge. Her hips
were two sharp blades. The Band-Aid bloomed red. For a
moment, Kate thought about climbing in beside her, the faucet pressing against her back, her daughter pressing against
her knees. But Leah didn't look at her—not pleadingly, or
searchingly, or any of the other things that eyes are said to
do—so she stayed where she was.

When it was time for Leah to leave home, she moved
across the country. She didn't have any particular reason—no
school, no job, no far-flung romance. A city she'd only ever
seen on postcards.

One night when they were still getting used to the empty

house, Kate slept in Leah's bed. She had a bad cough. Felix said he could sleep through anything, but she insisted. Her lungs burned and her ribs ached. She tossed and turned for hours. For a moment when she woke up—how had she finally fallen asleep?—she had no idea where she was. In daylight, her body seemed huge in the narrow bed. The quilt was clearly made for a child. Felix came and sat on the edge of the mattress, like a dad. They stayed that way for a while, not speaking, looking around the room as if it were a museum, or a dream.

She got better—it was just a cough—but after that the room was a little frightening. When Felix suggested they renovate the kitchen, Kate consumed herself with the details of transformation. Blueprints and paint chips, ten different kinds of door handles.

Construction began. Kate wanted to stay and watch, but Felix said the pleasure would be in the surprise—how much could change in the course of a single day. Old walls disappeared between breakfast and dinner, and by the next night new ones had appeared. They saw what was underneath the floorboards for the first time. Holes were filled with glass. One evening, they came home and the wallpaper had been installed upside down. The pattern was simple and geometric—it was admittedly not so clear which side was up. They left it that way. Soon enough, they liked it better that way.

Leah called on Sundays. Most of the time, Felix picked up on the first ring. She told him about her job and her girl-friend, about the community garden around the block—the tomatoes and the gladiola and the two orange hens. Kate learned the details afterward, whenever Felix told her. She pictured the hens with their bulging chests, their dinosaur feet. He couldn't remember the girlfriend's name.

"Did you even ask?" she said.

"It isn't always good to ask."

The next week, he put Leah on speakerphone in the middle of a sentence, and her voice filled up the empty kitchen. Kate and Felix looked at the phone between them. It was surprisingly easy to forget that it didn't really contain anything. Kate wanted to know if the hens laid eggs.

"I don't sound like myself," Leah said.

There were too many hard, clean surfaces. Kate looked from the phone to Felix. Leah's grey eyes and yellow eyelashes. She didn't want to say the wrong thing. *Eggs?* she mouthed.

"I'm hearing my own echo."

The fridge was still in plastic, silver and unsmudged. There was a sink-shaped hole in the counter.

"I'll take you to a different room," Felix said. "With softer things."

He carried the phone into the hall, the voice coming out of his palm, tinny and getting quieter, then gone.

ACKNOWLEDGMENTS

This book began in my head, where it would have remained were it not for the people who understood what it might be, who insisted on its becoming. Some of them have marked up these pages with pen; all of them have marked my work with their support.

Bill Clegg wrote the email that said *send the rest,* and changed everything. He is my guide, my guardian. Annie Bishai edited these stories with all her heart, which made them better, but also deeper. Kishani Widyaratna and Gillian Fitzgerald-Kelly brought them across an ocean. The entire team at The Clegg Agency and at Knopf—especially Simon Toop, David Kambhu, Victoria Pearson, John Gall, Amy Hagedorn, Elizabeth Bernard, and Morgan Fenton, and many whose work was invisibly invaluable—helped the book take flight and land safely.

Versions of these stories have appeared in *The New Yorker, Harper's, The Paris Review,* and *Electric Literature.*

Willing Davidson, Christopher Beha, Emily Nemens, and Halimah Marcus edited them with generosity and grace.

Henry Finder and David Remnick do with words and ideas what I admire most: they open up worlds. Mine is wider because of them. Jess Henderson, Leily Kleinbard, Sharan Shetty, David Wallace, Hannah Wilentz, and R. L. Lipstein have taught me so much about what a story is.

The teachers and students at the NYU Creative Writing Program first made me doubt that I could write a book, then helped me believe it.

Navy, Emily, Emma, Lucy, Zanny, and Dylan are true compasses, truer friends. Alice understands more than anyone the joy of playing pretend. Ben is my oldest coach and most loyal fan.

Eddie is everywhere—in the margins of every book, on the other side of every dream. I'm always writing you a letter.

My parents taught me to read and write—and then, to revise. Their patience and wisdom and love make all the difference.

For turning a work of fiction into something real: thank you all.

A Note About the Author

Clare Sestanovich is an editor at *The New Yorker*. Her fiction has appeared in *The New Yorker*, *The Paris Review*, *Harper's*, and *Electric Literature*. She lives in Brooklyn.

A *Note on the Type*

The text of this book was set in Electra, a typeface designed by W. A. Dwiggins (1880–1956). This face cannot be classified as either modern or old style. It is not based on any historical model, nor does it echo any particular period or style. It avoids the extreme contrasts between thick and thin elements that mark most modern faces, and it attempts to give a feeling of fluidity, power, and speed.

Composed by North Market Street Graphics, Lancaster, Pennsylvania
Printed and bound by LSC Communications, Harrisonburg, Virginia
Designed by Maria Carella